DARK TRUTH

DARK DESIRES
BOOK FIVE

SUMMER COOPER

LOVY BOOKS

Lovy Books Ltd
20-22 Wenlock Road
London N1 7GU

Cover by SC Creative

EMILY

"Are you ready to open it, Emily?" Dylan's voice above me broke the peaceful quiet I'd wrapped myself in. "It might wreak havoc, but you have me. I'm here with you."

Where you belong, I thought to myself. I snuggled closer for a moment longer, and then I pulled away. I wasn't a weak schoolgirl who needed a man to hold my hand through life. I did need a partner who would be there with me, though. I took a deep breath, sat up straight, and looked up into the most beautiful gray eyes I'd ever seen.

"I am. Let's see what Mister High and Mighty has in store now." I took the envelope from him, no bigger than a birthday card, and not too thick, and let my feet slide to the floor. I'd changed when I came home earlier, a pair of black shorts and a long white t-shirt.

I stared down at my turquoise blue toenails and held my breath. I had to do this the same way I'd rip a Band-Aid off, quickly and with no emotion. I inhaled, stuck my finger in the gap in the flap, and ripped it open. I took out the contents, and found two pages of typed paper. It was the thick kind my family used in their business operations, and I could see the words Thompson Resorts running through the grain.

Handwritten on cheap printer paper would have been warmer than this cold communication, but it was Trent. I wasn't even surprised to see his name signed at the bottom of page two, the same as he'd sign any business communication. I looked over at Dylan with doubt, but brought page one to the front to start to read.

"Dear Emily," I read aloud, "I hope you open this letter, because I've been a real jerk and need to apologize."

My words stuttered to a halt, and I glanced over at Dylan, my eyes narrowed. "A trick, you think?"

"I … don't know, Emily. You know your brother better than I do." He pulled me to him, and I cuddled into his side. The worst of it was over now. I needed his warmth to calm the surge of adrenaline that had rushed through me.

I'd expected another gut-wrenching letter, and my stomach was still in a defensive knot. Trent was either sorry, or he was trying a new tactic. I didn't trust this one bit.

"What else does he say?" Dylan asked, his chin on the top of my head.

"Um, he says he talked with his wife about it all, and that she nearly tore his head off. I don't doubt that, but why a letter? Why didn't she call me after this revelation?"

"Did she know?" he asked, his fingers on my shoulder.

"She must have; how else would he have explained blackballing me from the family?" I turned my head enough to look up at him and found our lips pressed together instead.

That made me giggle, and I kissed him properly before I turned back to the paper. "I've watched the children you used to take care of … ah, I get it—they need a babysitter."

"Maybe not, sweetheart, give it a chance." He nudged me a little, and I read on.

"The kids all miss their aunt, the wives miss their friend." That made me pause and snort with laughter. "The wives miss their friend? They missed me so much they forgot my birthday?"

"Emily…" Dylan dragged out my name, and I sighed.

"I know, I know. Let's see, oh right. Your mother and our father miss you. I have to admit, even I miss you. It's strange not having you around to kick me into gear when I need it." Another sigh. "Again, it's about how they feel. Not what they've put me through."

I'd let the paper fall to my lap and stared up at the ceiling. "They haven't learned."

"They're starting to, though, Emily. Writing that must have taken a lot for a man like Trent. Well, the man as I've experienced him, and you've explained him to me."

"He's not the most, um, gallant of men, no." My brother could be a self-righteous asshole of the highest order, actually.

"Give them all a chance."

I didn't want to, though. Trent hadn't even given me a chance to explain the situation. Although, to be fair, I hadn't really sought out a chance to do that. I'd avoided him. I shouldn't have, but I knew even then that Dylan was important to me, and well, now I knew that I loved him. I wanted this to work, and Trent was a threat to that. I didn't want to let him back into my life. Not if he was going to go off and do something like this again.

"Maybe he's seen the error of his ways?" Even I could hear the doubt in Dylan's voice and looked up at him, a little miffed.

"Why are you defending him so much? The man tried to keep you out of the business here." I stared at him and saw his face twist a little.

"It's not easy for me, you know? As you said, he gave me hell too. He's your brother, and family is important. I never had brothers or sisters, and it was probably best I didn't. When I was a kid, though, I always wanted a brother. Someone to play with when I was lonely."

"Are you really buying this then?" I waved the paper to show what I meant.

"I don't know, Emily." He sighed and shifted to sit up on the sofa. "I don't trust him for a minute, but like I said, you know him best. Would he try to play some trick on you like that?"

"He would," I said without a second of doubt. I'd grown up with him, and the man he was around Jessi wasn't the same man he was around his family. He could be ruthless, mean, and downright dirty when he wanted to be; not with Jessi.

"Then take some time and think about it. For tonight"—Dylan paused to take the letter from me—"let me feed you to dinner, and you can relax for a bit. You look tired. Do you want to stay in and order something?"

"Let's order food. I look grubby, and I don't want to see anyone but you tonight." I leaned against him, and he took me in his arms.

Immediately, the world faded away, and there was only Dylan's face and the safety of his arms. I relaxed and sighed. "Maybe we can try out that hot tub."

"Now that sounds like a plan. Let me order food, and we'll get set up."

I went out to make sure everything was right for a dip, the air was still a bit chilly but not bad, and then went into the kitchen. I cleaned out the pot the pasta had caught fire in and the rest of the dishes. I wasn't used to this kind of life, but I wasn't a bad cook. I'd had too much on my mind with that stupid letter, and I'd let Trent get to me. I shouldn't have allowed that, but I had.

I didn't know what to do about the mess my brother had put me in. He'd said he was sorry, wanted to rebuild our ties to each other. He wanted to meet us both, Dylan and I, over dinner to talk things through. Maybe Jessi had smoothed things over, but it still nagged at me that she hadn't called. Trent could have given her the number, or she could have contacted me on social media. I hadn't changed any of that.

I hadn't heard from any of them, though. I was persona non grata, and they'd let me know it, all of them. Until I'd started to move on with my life. Now that Dylan and I had agreed to share a home and our lives together, they'd decided to come back. As always, it was on their terms too.

Trent wanted to meet us. He didn't ask me if I'd like to meet or where. He'd just said, I'd like to meet you over dinner. I realized I'd been drying the same pot for a very long time and put it down. Yet again, Trent was interrupting my life.

I wanted to celebrate the new life I had with Dylan and, for tonight, my family could wait. I had a new person in my life, a new life, and he'd earned every bit of my love and trust. He'd pushed me over the edge of endurance sometimes, he'd pushed me to be *more* every single day, and I loved him for it.

He could have given up, said fuck it, and walked away when I didn't want to sign contracts. He could've found someone more willing to do what he wanted for the money he offered, but I'd never been in it for the money. I'd been in it for pleasure and nothing more. He'd sensed that, knew it, and together we'd created something worth fighting for.

I would fight my family if it came down to it, I would refuse to see any of them, if it was a choice between them and Dylan. They'd shown me their colors, and Dylan's hadn't run. I owed it to him to let this go for tonight. He had his own demons to face down, and we had work to do. We'd do them both, together.

I poured two glasses of chilled white wine and took them into his office. It was simply decorated, a small desk, his laptop, and a couch. A couch that needed breaking in, I thought with a dirty smirk. "Get something ordered?"

Dylan pushed away from his chair, his Oxford shirt

open at the throat, and the charcoal gray trousers begging to be opened. He held his arms out to me, and I went to him. I knelt in front of him, eager to please and ready for his love. "I did, darling. Your favorite Chinese will be here shortly."

"Oh, that sounds yummy, but I know something that tastes like heaven, right here at home." I let my fingers trail down the zipper of his trousers and licked my lips. My eyes were on his face, and I watched his gaze flick between my fingers and my lips with satisfaction. He was tempted then.

"There's nothing more I'd like than to watch your lips wrap around my dick, Emily, but they'll be here soon. I think we should wait." His fingers slid along mine, and I pressed them into the rigid length beneath his zipper, belying his words.

"Darling," I pouted with a wet smile. "I've thought about it all day long."

Not a lie. I always had Dylan and sex in the back of my mind somewhere.

"You can wait another hour, pet." His tongue darted out for a moment, but dragged it a little across his bottom lip on the way back in. He wanted to taste me, and I felt a response deep between my thighs.

"If I must." I squeezed a little harder on his length, then stood. I leaned over to kiss him before he could respond. Our lips met with a passion that hadn't dimmed at all, and he inhaled deeply. I felt his fingers run up my face and into my hair, as he deepened the kiss and turned it into something that was so much hotter.

I moaned into his mouth and pulled him up from the chair. Our lips never parted as I backed up against the wall. With a groan of resignation, filled with desire, Dylan picked me up and pressed me into the wall. I felt him pressing into me in just the right way and wrapped my legs around him with glee.

He broke the kiss and looked down at me. "You fucking little tease. You just want to get off before you eat, don't you?"

"You know me well, sir." I looked up at him from beneath my lashes, but smiled that dirty smile he'd taught me.

"If that's what you want, I don't mind meeting the delivery boy with your scent all over my face."

Something clenched inside of me, and I screamed with joy when he turned and dropped me on the desk. He stripped my shorts away as he knelt in front of me, spread my legs, and found the part of me that ached the most for him with his tongue.

"Dylan…" I sighed his name, my fingers in his hair. My head fell back, and I ground into him as his tongue worked at me. Quickly, and with an expert touch, Dylan's tongue slicked over my clit, until my hips danced on the edge of the desk.

My legs were hitched over his shoulder, and I wanted to lean back, but the desk wasn't wide enough. I had to make do with pressing my palms into the oak top and writhing against him. It wouldn't take long, not when he wanted to make me come quickly. It never did, because he knew exactly what I liked.

"Baby, Dylan, fuck, make me come. Please." It wasn't necessary to beg, but the words came out just the same. He didn't bother to answer, except to slide two fingers inside of me. As soon as he did, my walls went tight around his fingers, and my breath stopped. I could feel it, just out of reach. Just a little more … and then his fingers began to slide in and out of me, in time with his tongue.

"That's it, fuck, that's it, Dylan." The world exploded, and I gave myself up to the first explosion.

He didn't stop. He made sure the job was done right, and carried on until I begged him to let it end. That was about the time we heard the doorbell going. Our food was here.

Dylan stood, wiped his face, smirked at me and went to get the food. I put my shorts on as I listened to the exchange in the hallway with wobbly legs. I wondered if he'd consent to videoing that. I'd love to watch the whole thing from the outside, so to speak. The way he touched me, the way I responded. I considered it as I went into the kitchen. He was there, and I went up to kiss him.

I could smell my scent on him, and from the look in his eyes, I knew I'd have to eat quickly. He was ready for far more than cunnilingus on his office desk, and I was more than willing to satisfy. We didn't have a playroom here. We'd gone beyond that kind of thing and could go to Elmo's for that if we wanted it. Which gave me another idea, one I'd discuss with him later. When the thought of letting others watch me would drive him mad with desire.

2

———————

EMILY

I thought about that letter off and on over the next two weeks. I really wanted to just forget the whole thing and let it go, but something wouldn't let me. Maybe it was that part of me had once been a little girl who looked up to her older brother. Or the grown woman who wanted to be seen. I wasn't sure, but I couldn't let it go. I knew I should make a decision, and I knew Dylan would support whatever I decided.

That didn't mean I wanted to, though. There was also a part of me that said, let them all stew for a while. I wasn't normally vindictive, but I wasn't perfect either. Something ugly and mean in me said they needed to learn. They hadn't learned when I'd made it clear I was unhappy. They hadn't learned when I point-blank said that they took me for granted. No, they'd just gone on as if I hadn't said anything at all.

Well, now they'd know what it was like to wonder and to worry maybe.

I went about my job and lived through each day as much as I could with happiness. Three days had now passed since I'd read the stupid thing, and I was a bundle of nerves I screeched when my phone buzzed. It had been so quiet, and I'd been so engrossed in my thoughts that the sound startled me.

"Hello?" I said, even though I knew it was Dylan. I slid my Louboutin heels off and smiled. "What can I do for you, handsome?"

"I'm your superior, my dear. Shouldn't you call me sir, or Mr. James, perhaps?" His voice purred down the line, and my head swiveled into my shoulder with glee.

"Mm, I probably should. Maybe you should come up here and instruct me on how to answer your calls properly?" My voice was breathy, a sound I'd cringe at if I ever used it on anyone but Dylan. Although, he had said I'd make a fortune as a phone sex operator. I wasn't sure those were still a thing, but he knew best.

"I'd do you one better, pet. Pack a bag or two. I'm going to take you away for the weekend. Back to that little cabin in the woods. Where I can teach you so many things, pet, so many things."

"Oh, that sounds like fun, sir. I'm not sure I want to go away this weekend. Maybe I'd like to stay home."

"I think you'll do as I say, pet." His voice became

stern, quiet, but only because someone must have entered the room. Otherwise, he'd have remained playful.

"Where are you?" I asked, curiously.

"I'm at Elmo's. I needed Roxie to arrange a few things for me."

"Hmm. Now what could Roxie possibly arrange for you, Dylan?" I wondered if it had anything to do with the things I'd said to him a few nights ago.

"Things, my dear. Now, pack your bags like a good girl. Don't be difficult."

"Of course not, sir. I will be ready." He hadn't said a time, but that didn't matter. I hung up the phone and went up to our penthouse. I loaded a travel bag with the clothes I'd need up there: a pair of jeans, some under-wear, and a sweatshirt. I packed a warm nightgown, just in case, and added a few pair of socks.

There was a washer if I needed to wash my clothes, but I knew I'd barely have any on the entire time we were there. There were robes, food, a few other things up there, in case anyone needed them. I packed my toiletries, medicine, and a laptop. I might want to watch a movie or something on the plane. Once we were there, Dylan would keep me busy.

I laid down on the bed, suddenly flooded with fatigue. I'd only packed a bag, but it was late in the day, and I hadn't slept well the night before. I only meant to close my eyes against the afternoon sunlight, but when I woke up, the room was dark and Dylan was standing over me.

"You ready, Emily?" he asked softly.

"Yes, sorry, let me just run to the bathroom." I pushed up, brushed my hair out of my face, and ran to the bathroom.

It took ten minutes, then we were ready to go. I had my hiking boots on, my hair was tied up, and I wore a long black sweatshirt over my jeans. I was ready to go, but my brain was still sluggish. I fell asleep on Dylan as the plane took off a short while later.

He woke me up as the plane landed. I was a little refreshed now and looked around the route happily as he drove us up to the cabin.

"I'd started to think you were going to sleep through the whole trip. Are you alright?" He looked concerned but kept his gaze on the road.

He was always a careful driver.

"I'm fine. Probably just stress. I didn't sleep well last night."

"That's why we're coming up here. I thought you'd need a break from worrying about your family. It won't be long, and we'll be so far away from them they'll never find you."

I wanted to say he didn't know my family, but it would only sound snotty, and I didn't want that. It was only a few more minutes before he pulled up to the cabin. The lights had been left on for us, and a note and the keys were on the counter by the sink.

"They hope we enjoy our stay, and they'll send up a cleaner when we're done. We're not to worry about anything," I said to Dylan as he carried in the bags.

"It's not that big, so it's not a problem to clean up before we go," he said, but I knew he was only talking to himself. He set the bags down and shut the door behind him. "Now, get that bath going, and let's have a nice, hot soak."

"You check the fire. I learned how cold it can be when we get out of the bath the last time we were here," I said over my shoulder and heard Dylan chuckle.

I went into the bathroom and found a nice selection of candles. I lit a few and turned the tap on. It wouldn't take long for the bath to heat up. I went and found a couple of towels and the robes, and draped them over the sink, then went out to turn down the bed. It was covered in a thick down duvet, with a white duvet cover and white sheets. It was rather cold to look at, but so heavenly to slip into.

I went into the bathroom and undressed. I was about to slip into the water when Dylan came in.

"Sneaky, getting in before me so you can stretch out." His smile took the edge off the accusation.

"You know it, baby." I grinned and slid into the

bathtub carefully. When I was in, I stretched carefully, letting my hair absorb the water as the heat relaxed every muscle in my body for a moment.

He left me to relax, and as hungry as my body was for him, it also needed to relax. I heard the soft sound of music begin to play, some kind of soft jazz that we both found we liked, just to fill the air with sound. I thought about that as I soaked in the tub, how we humans always needed sound to soothe us. So many people craved quiet, and I did sometimes. Then, at other times, it just seemed to cause distress and we had to fill it.

Dylan was perceptive. He knew that quiet would allow me time to dance around the questions in that letter. He knew I needed peace, but maybe not so much of the quiet, and I loved him even more for it. I still couldn't comprehend that my brother had thought so badly of the man. Yes, he could be the world's biggest dick when it came to business, but in relationships? There wasn't anyone I'd rather have in my life than him, obviously.

I sank deeper into the hot water with a sigh full of bliss.

"Mind if I join you now?"

I opened my eyes to see the stunning image of Dylan's naked body poised over the tub. It was time to play.

3

EMILY

The next day Dylan and I bundled up and went for a walk in the woods. It wasn't exactly cold, but there was a chilly breeze, and a few places along the path were filled with shadows that were still damp from snow. We strolled hand in hand and talked as we walked through the trees and shrubs that grew wild around the cabin.

"What if we just bought a cabin of our own out here and ran away from city life? Left all of that modern stuff behind and just went about our business?" Dylan surprised me by saying.

"What? You've finally got what you wanted, a resort in Myrtle Beach..." The words trailed off, and I stopped to look at him.

Dylan pulled me tight against the wall of muscle that

was his abdomen and leaned down to kiss my neck. "What if what I want has changed?"

I laughed, delighted at the words and his kisses. "Dylan…"

"We'll talk about it later," Dylan purred the words and gently pushed me back against a massive tree. I let my head fall against the rough bark of the blackgum tree and was on the verge of an answer when his lips came down on mine.

There was something almost frantic about his kiss. It lacked the calm of the way he normally kissed me, and urgency took hold. His sudden need to have every inch of me pressed into him sparked a reaction inside of me, and I wound my arms around his neck to pull my body closer to his.

We'd spent weeks, months together now, but there were times when it might have been the very first time we'd touched. This was one of those times, and I rode the intensity of Dylan's passion to a place where mine matched his exactly.

His hands slid under the sweatshirt I'd thrown on and found my breasts free of any other garments. It was one of the reasons I liked being up here; I didn't need to wear a bra constantly. I heard a pleased hum from him when his cold fingers found the warm skin of my naked nipples. Then it was me that did the humming as his fingers teased the taut peaks until I squirmed against him.

His lips moved down my neck, and I gasped his name. The sunlight had started to fade, but I didn't care how the shadows grew; all I cared about was the way he made me feel. His hand pushed my shirt up, and his hot mouth found my nipples. I felt the tug of his lips and groaned as need pulsed through me.

His fingers moved around to the back of my pants, before I felt the cold touch of his fingers on my skin. I opened my eyes, but I knew there wasn't anyone around that would see us. I just wanted to make sure this was real. "Dylan … I…"

He cut my words off with a searing kiss, one that took my breath away. I thought he'd strip me down, turn me around, and take me there against the tree. Instead, he picked me up and with confident strides, he carried me into the house and dropped me softly onto the bed. My clothes were peeled away by skillful hands and before I knew it, he had me on my hands and knees.

I expected quick and rough, but Dylan touched me with gentle fingers that traced down the slim line of my spine. I arched up into that touch, but he carried on. His fingers splayed over the globes of my ass, and I heard him kneel behind me. I was completely naked, and he was totally clothed.

"I don't think I can live without you anymore,

Emily." I thought I heard him say, but it was so soft, he might have said something else. Maybe it was wishful thinking on my part and he hadn't really said that at all.

My heart skipped a few beats, and I was about to ask him to repeat himself, when his tongue slid onto me. I groaned again, greedy for more. I knew from experience, though, that more wouldn't be enough. Even when he drove me over the edge over and over again, it was never enough. Even when I begged him to let me have a moment to breathe, I couldn't wait for more.

I reached back because I needed to touch him, and found his hair. I tugged at the silky strands and moaned when he moved away.

"Problem, Emily?" he asked, always attentive to me.

"No, I just, I just wanted to touch you, Dylan." I pulled away from him and turned to rest on my back. "Come to me."

I felt odd saying, but it seemed to be the right words for the moment.

"As you wish, my dear." He crawled over me and propped himself up on his elbows over my face. "I love looking at you, you know?"

I looked into the gray of his eyes and felt something squeeze, hot and tight, in my chest. "You've got a face worth staring at."

It was a pathetic response, but I couldn't tell him what I really wanted to say, could I? Dylan was many things, but he wasn't the 'I love you' kind of man. It might even make him run away, kick me out of the new penthouse, and never speak to me again. I pushed away the emotion and concentrated on the moment instead.

He was real, between my thighs and over me, and that was all I wanted. All I'd wanted for a long time now. I didn't want to spoil the moment or our relationship and admit to having feelings for him that he might not return. He cared about me, I knew that by now, but I doubted he'd ever really admit that he loved me. I could live with that.

"Show me how much you like looking at me, Dylan," I purred the words in a way I knew he couldn't resist. It was a voice I'd learned drove him, the tone pitched just right to distract him from whatever he was doing. It was a signal to him, and it worked now, the same as it always did.

There were no more words, just the sensation of being sweetly invaded as Dylan drove into me in one sure, swift thrust that left us both gasping. I stared up at him, my body tangled in his, and tried to give him my love with my eyes. When he slid along a particularly sweet spot, my eyes closed.

I clutched his strong body as he rocked into me with strong thrusts timed expertly. He knew exactly what I needed and how I needed it. Dylan knew exactly where to touch me, which buttons to push, as his hands softly explored my body. I was aware of the delicate way he touched my shoulder, the way he rocked my hips up to meet his, and learned all over again what it felt like to be aware of every part of my body.

Dylan's touch drove me into a place only he could take me to. I might not have had very much experience with men, but I had plenty of experience with a real man. It was all I needed to know, all I ever wanted to know.

He sighed with languid enjoyment as he drove into me again, deeper, a little harder. "You fit around me like a glove, Emily. A glove I never want to take off."

"I'm made for you, Dylan, nobody else," I assured him, my nails clutched into his back.

I felt them drag across his skin as he began a deeper pace that was a little faster. It stole my breath away as the slick slide of him inside of me touched places that ached for his stimulation. I moved with him, my hips in tune with his, a dance that we'd perfected and enhanced.

He moved and arched my back so that my nipples were within easy reach, and sucked hard at the left one.

"Dylan…" I called his name, but he didn't answer; he only sucked harder. The sensation of his lips as they tugged at my nipples reminded me of those little sucking torture devices he sometimes placed on me. They drove me up the wall, but they felt so fucking good. I loved every second of it when he put them on me, and I longed for them now.

His lips were just as stimulating, though, and I thrust my breasts higher so that he'd have easy access to the nipple. My hips took over the pace, and I thrust up into him, my body not my own now. It was its own being, and all it wanted was pleasure. "Make me come, Dylan, please."

Instead of answering, he used a free hand to guide my fingers down to the wet folds of my pussy. I found the spot I needed to have touched the most and ran a finger over it. Just a tease at first, but when I knew I was in the right spot, I applied pressure. In well-timed circles, I matched the pace of my hips, and within minutes I felt the first pulse rock through me.

"That's it, Dylan. Harder. Please, harder." I panted as I demanded my pleasure, and when he bit down lightly on the tight bud of my nipple, that gentle rock became a crushing wave. My back arched impossibly tighter, and my throat closed around a scream. It felt as if I would blow apart, as if my entire body would just shut down, as if I had indeed died a little death, but it felt so good. I didn't want it to stop, as waves pulsed through me, all the way up to my brain and down again as my walls clutched around him.

I knew the strong orgasm would make my walls milk Dylan, and I wasn't surprised when I heard him groan. For a moment he went still, and I felt the small pulse all over again. Only this time, it was Dylan's cock that had pulsed inside of me, but it didn't stop the full onslaught of waves that crashed through me all over again.

"Emily..." he choked out as he slammed himself inside of me, hard and deep. I clutched him to me, my fingers on his ass, my nails digging into his skin. His ass was so round and perfect, my fingers often found their way there when he was naked. It was instinctual to touch him there, to urge him to curve deeper into me as he came apart.

We clung together after, our bodies exhausted for now. He rolled away with a soft groan but pulled me to him. I rolled to throw a leg over his hip and put my head on his shoulder.

"Why do you feel so good, Emily?" His eyes were closed, but his right hand was on my head, holding me there gently. "I can't get you out of my system, no matter how many times I fuck you. It just makes me want you more."

"I don't know," I answered softly, unsure of what to say. "I only know you, Dylan, and I don't want to know anyone else."

"That's good, because I can tell you right now—I'd kill any other man that tried to touch you." I heard the growl in his voice and knew he meant it.

"Even if we were at Elmo's?" It was a gamble to ask, but I'd hinted at it before.

"That would be," he paused, and put his right arm over his eyes. "Fuck, that makes me hard all over again, but I don't know if I could do it. Watch another man whip you, touch you…"

"Or fuck me?" I finished the sentence. It was something I'd hinted at before, but like him, it wasn't something I was positive I wanted.

"Sometimes it's good to fantasize. Not so good when it happens." He moved his arm to look up at me, his face clear of most emotions. All I could see was concern there.

"I know, and that's my fear. It's always been my fear when I try to make fantasies reality."

"It worked out alright with me," Dylan countered, just to play Devil's advocate.

"True, but as you just said, fantasy isn't always what you get with reality."

"Not always, no." He put his arm down and placed it over my hip. "We can try it, if you're that curious. I would never stop you from trying new things. I can't promise I won't lose my shit if another man touches you, but I can try. I owe you that."

"Why do you owe me that?" I asked, and pulled away to look at him.

"Because, you gave me your virginity. You didn't

know I was going to monopolize your time when you did that."

"I *like* that you monopolize my time, Dylan. I don't have a problem with that, at all."

"What about other women? Would that be satisfying?" There was a gentle purr to his voice when he asked.

"I don't know. I'm not against it, but I'm not sure I want it either?" I looked at him again, and then finished. "Besides, wouldn't a woman touching me be the same as a man?"

"You might be on to something there, my dear. Do you want some juice?" he asked and rolled off the bed.

I heard a glass break in the kitchen and called out to Dylan. He called back and said he'd knocked a glass on the shelf and to stay in the bedroom while he cleaned it up.

I went to the bathroom, freshened myself up with a quick shower, and then went back to bed. Dylan came in with two glasses of juice and handed me one.

"What do you want to eat tonight? We have that roast in the freezer, or we can have something quick? I can pop some of that fried chicken into the oven."

Dylan liked to do most of the cooking while we were here. At home he rarely had time to do it, but here, he had all the time in the world.

"The chicken sounds nice." I plopped back onto the

pillows and rolled up in a ball. Wake me up when it's done."

"Lazy-bones," I heard Dylan say, but just chuckled. I was very tired suddenly, and I wasn't kidding when I told him to wake me up because I was hungry too. Which was another reason I chose the chicken; it wouldn't take as long to cook as the roast.

I closed my eyes, and my thoughts drifted away. Soon enough, I was asleep, and the world no longer existed outside of my brain's impulses. When I woke up an hour later, Dylan was at the foot of the bed with a grin.

"KFC has nothing on me, baby. Come on, let's eat." Dylan pulled me up when I put my hand out to him, and I soon found myself at a small dining table. He had mashed potatoes, macaroni and cheese, and green beans spread in bowls around the chicken.

"It looks great." It was only frozen fried chicken, but it was a gourmet variety and tasted surprisingly good.

"Thanks. I made the macaroni and cheese myself, by the way." The cabin's fridge and chest freezer were always stocked up. Dylan would have found anything he needed in those or the pantry.

"It's delicious," I said around a mouthful of hot mac and cheese. I saw him smile in pleasure and felt my own little smidgeon of delight as he did. Dylan wasn't necessarily used to compliments, but he was getting used to mine.

"What are we going to do now?" I asked when we'd finished eating and had cleaned up.

"Well, we can watch a movie, read a book, or just sit on the couch together and stare out at the stars in the sky." We wouldn't be able to see a lot from the couch, even with the lights off, but it would be nice.

"The last one," I said and slipped over to the wall to turn off the light.

We settled onto the couch; Dylan's arms were around me, and I closed my eyes, enjoying the moment. I'd put on a robe to eat dinner and was glad. There, in the dark, it was a little chilly, even with the fire going.

"What did you want to be when you were little? Before life got in the way, and Trent was such an asshole to you?" His words were almost like a splash of cold water on the fantasy-land I'd found myself in. I thought about his question, though, rather than letting it ruin the moment.

"I wanted to be an astronaut." As soon as the word left my mouth a raucous laughter burst from Dylan's lips. "Stop laughing!" I pushed against his side, and he stopped chuckling.

"Really? You'd want to leave this world behind?" He looked genuinely curious, and I looked up at the stars beyond the tips of the tallest trees outside.

"I did. I wanted to look at the planet from the other side and explore other worlds. I wanted to see if the Crab Nebula really was that bright and beautiful. I wanted to see Mars from close up, and walk on the moon." I heard the wistfulness in my voice.

"It sounds amazing, you're right. Why didn't you?"

"I'm a Thompson. It's that simple. We don't leave the world behind. I had the grades for it, and I could have worked to make sure I was NASA material, but, well, I'm a Thompson. We do hotels, not space rockets."

"I understand." He hugged me tight and apologized for laughing.

"No, it's alright. It's a man's job, right?"

"Not at all. I've just never met someone with such high, um, dreams."

"I don't expect many people have." It was a crazy idea, but one I still sometimes thought about.

"If you were offered the opportunity, would you go into space?" he asked a few moments later.

"I might. If I hadn't found you." I snuggled deeper into his side and didn't think about what I'd admitted too much.

Dylan had changed my life in a million ways, and I was still finding out what some of those ways were. It wasn't his fault that I wouldn't go into space now, it was my own. I'd stopped myself from that dream a long time ago, but I had a really good reason to stay put on the planet now. I'd stay right here on Earth. With him.

"I don't want to hold you back, Emily. From anything, but I'm happy you feel that way." His fingers tangled into my hair, and I moved my head up to meet his. Our lips merged together, and I deepened the kiss into something far more passionate. I moved over him as he slid to his back, and I put my arms on each side of his head.

Our hips danced together, despite the fact that he'd put pants on, and our hands began to explore. We should have probably got off the couch and went to the bed, but I liked being on top of him. I pressed my hips down into the hard length between us, the tip pushed into my clit in just the right way, and I groaned.

Dylan moved my head away so that he could nip at my neck just below my ear.

"Even this blows my mind Emily. I'm not even inside of you, and it feels too good to stop."

"Even for second?" I breathed out raggedly.

"Even for a second, baby. Even knowing I'd get the glory that is that sweet, wet pussy of yours. Fuck, don't stop," he groaned when I slowed my pace.

It only took a slip of my hand and a quick push up, and then I was sliding down his hard length that was only mine. I lost myself in him and forgot about the world outside, one more time.

4

____

EMILY

Our time at the cabin replayed in my mind a few days later. I was in my office, in the staff area hidden away on the first floor, and the sun was steaming into my window. It reminded me of how the sun would stream into the window behind the couch, and how I loved to stare out of that window. I'd always been a city girl, but I loved it out there.

The fact that it was also the only time we were out of complete contact with the world was a factor in how much I loved the place. The rest was just how peaceful it was out there. No cars zoomed by to make noise, there were no buses, large trucks, screaming children, arguing couples; nothing but the scenery and the wildlife we sometimes spotted. It was quiet, and life was slow. I missed that sometimes, especially on the days when life was so hectic. Like today.

Already, I'd gone through two dozen cover letters and resumes with Michelle Gilder, the woman Dylan hired to run the Human Resources for the resort. I rolled my eyes at a cover letter that only contained the word hi and nothing else. Some of the emailed cover letters and resumes were so bad we didn't get past the cover letter. I didn't exactly have a defined job at the resort, and for the moment that was fine with me. I was able to see how everything worked and got to know the staff as they came along.

"I know a few of these people," Michelle said with a tired smile. "They are good people and need jobs, so I've already decided to hire them."

"That makes this a little easier then. Dylan has a chef lined up, and he'll hire staff for the kitchens once he arrives. Right now, we need housekeeping, restaurant wait staff, and registration ."

"Don't forget managers," Michelle pointed out as we stared at the stack on the floor.

We'd both gone through the monumental task of printing off the resumes, and once we met up in my office we'd just settled onto the floor. I moved my leg, covered in gray jeans and a pair of tan leather boots, and kicked over a stack of papers I'd forgotten about.

"Damn, there's more of them," I said absently and picked up the stack to bring it to the pile we had in front of us. It was over a foot high.

"Why don't you go and get us some lunch, and I'll keep going," Michelle said without looking up.

I sighed as I stared at the pile we still needed to get through, but we needed to eat. My stomach had been a little queasy this morning, so I hadn't eaten anything, but I was full-on starving now.

Michelle told me what she wanted, and I walked off, phone in my hand. When I got to my car and plugged it into the car's system, I remembered I needed to make a call. A very important one that I couldn't believe I'd forgotten about!

I dialed the number as I waited in the long line of cars at the drive-thru.

"Hi, this is Emily Thompson. I need to schedule an appointment for my injection."

"Hi there, Miss Thompson! We've been trying to reach you."

"Have you? I thought I wasn't due for another few weeks or so." I wasn't exactly sure when it was due, the math had become jumbled in my head long ago. I wasn't used to taking birth control but had started before I met Dylan.

"Oh no, Miss Thompson, we tried to call you last month when you were due in. When you missed your appointment, we tried to call you."

"I changed my phone number," I said out loud as the thought dawned on me.

"Wait, last month?" Fuck, only in my head the dirty word stretched out for a few seconds. "Last month?"

My voice had gone tiny and flat, but the woman on the other end didn't seem to notice.

"Yes, do you want to come in today? You need to talk to the doctor, and we need to reschedule that shot."

"Uh, yeah, that might be a good idea." Add in a pregnancy test too I thought.

The world seemed to narrow down to a pinpoint in front of me, and I couldn't hear anything. Pregnant. I could be pregnant. Dylan was going to lose his mind. The one thing I'd said I'd taken care of, and had, I'd forgotten to continue.

He'd made it clear at the beginning that he wanted me on birth control. We'd discussed it quite openly and without any hesitation. I'd told him it was taken care of and now, it seemed I might have messed that up.

"Can you come in around four, Miss Thompson? We'll need to update your file too, so maybe come a little earlier." The woman's voice broke through the moment of panic, and I stared out at the cars in front of me that still hadn't moved.

"Sure, yeah." I shook my head and focused. "I can be there at four." I was supposed to meet Dylan for dinner later this evening but might have to miss that.

"Great, we'll see you then. Have a great day!"

I knew the woman at the doctor's office couldn't do

the panic thing with me. She couldn't tell me I was stupid and that I might have made the biggest mistake of my life. She couldn't tell me to just come in right now and get the panic over with. Not that I'd stop panicking if I was pregnant. In fact, I'd be terrified.

How the fuck would I be able to tell Dylan, when were only just getting past his discovery of who I was? Damn, why had I been so stupid? I should have made a note somewhere, or done something, anything, to make sure this wasn't a worry.

Cars finally moved and I pulled up, ordered the food Michelle and I wanted. I paid the guy at the window, and drove back to the resort, my movements robotic. There was nobody I could call, to tell me to unlock the death grip I had on the steering wheel, or to tell me I could do this all on my own.

I could be pregnant! I wanted to scream it out in my panicked state. I tried to hide it, and Michelle, bless her, tried to pretend she didn't notice something was wrong. Her face, faintly lined with age, highlighted by two brown eyes framed with brown curl, gazed at me with sympathy, but she didn't push. We weren't close like that.

I ate the food mechanically, even though I'd been starving for it less than an hour ago. What would I do if I was pregnant? I stuck a battered onion ring in my mouth and chewed, without tasting it. I had money, that wasn't a problem. I could take care of a child, support it. What worried me was if I was capable of taking care of a child on my own.

I had a feeling Dylan would freak out, expect the worse from me, and accuse me of trapping him. Like his father did his mother. A cold wash of dread coursed through me, and I stared out of the window of my office. Would he see me as no better than his mother?

It was an accident, a mistake I'd made. I'd forgotten that I'd changed my number and hadn't told the doctor's office. I'd meant to call them, to find out when I needed to come in, but the migraines started, and then we moved. Now, I didn't know what to do.

I didn't answer the phone when Dylan called me, and I wasn't really helpful to Michelle after that. I tried to text Dylan, but my brain was mostly blank. I couldn't tell him that I was terrified, although he was the one person that I should have been able to talk to. He was, in most matters, but this was a situation of truly fucked upon beyond all recognition proportions.

I tapped a nail against my lip and stared down at my phone. He wanted to know if I was good for our dinner plans. It was 3 pm. I needed to get ready to go to the doctor. I stuck my lip between my teeth with my nail. It was a good thing I had gel nails, or I'd have been chewing at the damn thing.

I hurriedly sent a text back, told him I had an

appointment at 4, but didn't elaborate. I ran up to the penthouse, showered, and took the elevator down to the car without looking at my phone. I didn't want to know what he might have asked. I didn't want to do this, my mind cried as I drove through the traffic out to the medical office. I didn't want to fill out the form, as I sat in the doctor's waiting room. I didn't want to pretend to be happy and cheerful with the receptionist.

I was imploding inside but tilted my head at the right time and brought out the southern charm as much as the girl at the desk did. I sat and watched some kind of soap opera and tried not to tap my foot while I waited. To be fair, I'd arrived ten minutes early. It was only right that I had to sit there for a few minutes and wait.

I wanted Dylan there, to hold his hand as I explained what had happened in the last few months, and why I hadn't come back in. Instead, I did it on my own. As I'm sure countless women have also done.

"Well, to be honest with you, Emily, I'd say there's a possibility that you are pregnant. I'm not sure why you were prescribed Topamax, you're a sexually active woman and there are clear indications it interferes with your birth control. Add to that, the fact that you missed a dose, and well, I think we need to do a test."

I wanted to scream no at her, to tell her it wasn't possible and to just give me a new shot, but I hung my head and meekly agreed. I peed in a cup, and not long later the doctor came back, her face blank.

"The test is positive, Emily." Her voice was as blank as my stare as the word *positive* sank through me.

"Positive?" Just like that, my entire world changed. I'd hoped it would be negative and hadn't let myself think about what the opposite result would mean beyond Dylan's response. Now, I knew there was a life growing inside of me.

"Yes. We need to discuss your options and where to go from here. If you need some time to think about it, I can reschedule you."

"That would be great," I said, but I didn't really need time to consider the options. I'd keep the baby, it was my baby, something I thought I'd never have. The baby hadn't been part of my plans, but, well, it was in my belly now.

Dread left me when I thought about it, and I knew then that whatever reaction Dylan had, I'd keep it. I'd have a child of my own, and that made everything different.

I left the office in a stupor of quiet happiness. I was going to have a baby. I couldn't stop smiling the whole way home. It was after five, so I had time to get ready for our dinner date at seven. I found the penthouse empty, so I changed, put on a loose, thin sweater in a weathered, coppery green color, slid on a flirty black skirt, threw an emerald green scarf around my neck, brushed my hair, grabbed the first pair of black heels that I came to, and left the apartment.

I was scared, terrified, but ready for whatever this dinner might bring. I tapped out a message to Dylan and told him I'd meet him at the restaurant. Surprisingly, he'd gone quiet now. I had to tell him, but was now the right time? I had no idea how far along I was—I must have zoned out when the doctor told me because I couldn't remember—it must be at least two weeks, or the test wouldn't have worked.

I blew air out through my lips as I pulled into the restaurant's parking area. I'd tell him, if I could see that the time was right. I just wasn't sure if there ever was a right time to drop something like that on someone. Sure, we'd agreed to live together, and we were happy together. I have a feeling we're in this for the long haul, maybe even forever, but would a child change that?

I brushed blond hair out of my face as I walked in through the glass doors and told the waiter I was meeting Dylan. The young man smiled and turned to lead me to Dylan's table. I didn't notice anything about the young man, all I could see was Dylan's smile.

I could tell that man anything, that smile said. I could get through any devastation with him by my side. This should be easy to tell him, but it wasn't. We hadn't discussed children, only birth control. Then there was his mom. His real mom. Would he hate me, would he react with gentleness, like his father, or would this send him over the edge, as it had his mother? I wish I knew, I thought, and bit the inside of my lip as I leaned over to kiss him hello. I really wish I knew how he'd react to the news I had to drop on him at some point.

5

DYLAN

I knew the moment she walked into the restaurant and looked up. I wasn't the least bit surprised to see her there. For a moment, I could see she was uncertain about something, but then, her focus changed and her face beamed. Maybe that was the one thing that really made my heart melt about that woman. She was always happy to see me. Really happy.

It made a difference in your life when you knew your presence changed a person's day. I'd known plenty of times that my presence made my employees nervous or angry, and I knew that my parents enjoyed having me with them, but knowing you made someone's, a woman's, day better was something I'd never thought I'd enjoy this much.

"Hi, Emily," I said to her as she leaned down to kiss me and took a seat.

"Hi, Dylan. How are you?" She looked me over, and I was glad my hands weren't shaking. She'd have spotted it. "You've had your hair cut. It looks good."

I touched my dark brown hair and felt my lips tilt. "It was getting too long."

"I liked being able to tug on it." Her eyes went wide and then narrowed down to let me know she was being provocative.

"Mm, perhaps you should sit closer, pet." I liked the way she would get turned on in public. It only took a moment, and she had been so adventurous lately that I wondered now what we could get away with in the dimly lit restaurant.

"Perhaps you should take me to Elmo's later." Her voice went quiet, but it held a challenge.

"Oh? Do you want to play, pet?" There was something different about her tonight. Mysterious.

"I might be up for a little play." She smiled, a smile that challenged me to play along.

"We'll see. Tonight, I think we need to talk about your brother's letter." I saw how she tensed, and that was exactly why I'd changed subjects. "I know you want to avoid this, Emily, and I understand why, but you need to make a decision about the whole affair."

She blinked at me, and I wasn't sure if it was only because of the sudden change of subject, or if she was angry with me. Emily didn't anger easily, not from my experience anyway, but there was always a first time.

"You're right." Emily reached for her wine glass, but then shifted her hand to her glass of water instead. "I really need to deal with my family, don't I?"

She didn't look up at me as she pulled her lip between her teeth. She took another sip of water, and I saw the gold rings on her finger glint in the dim light. She was in distress, but you wouldn't know it if you didn't know Emily well. The way she drank the water, slow and thoughtful, as if it was the last glass of water she'd ever have told me all I needed to know.

I cared about her, that was something I'd stopped denying to myself long ago. I knew this conversation wasn't easy for her, and maybe I would take her to Elmo's. It had been a while, and we always enjoyed our time there. It could be a treat for coming to a decision.

"Dylan, I want to…" Her words stopped, and blonde brows knitted together. They weren't as blonde as her hair, but a darker shade that complimented her eyes.

"Go on, you want what, my dear?" I wanted her to face the problem and come to a decision. I was glad to be there to help her make that decision. Even if she didn't want to do that yet. It was time.

She'd been very stressed since that letter came from Trent. She wanted to avoid confrontation, but she had to face facts. She would have no peace until she came to a decision about it, either way.

"I just want to know if he means it. It could be a trick, you know. To get me to tell him what you're doing or something." She held her hand out as if it held all the secrets of the world.

"Emily, you grew up with this man. You said he was a dick, but is he that much of a dick?" I winced because I knew what her words would be before she even spoke.

"He made my father disown me, Dylan." Her gaze was a little frosty, and I took her hand.

"Sorry, that was insensitive." I stroked her palm until her eyes cleared and then spoke again. "What shall we eat? Let's table the discussion for now and eat."

"The chicken looks nice. I'd really like some chicken." She hadn't even looked at the menu, but we'd been here before, and I saw her looking around at other tables.

"What about the roast lamb?" I offered, that was what I wanted.

Her eyes went wide, and she turned a little green. "What's wrong, Emily?"

"No, lamb. Oh, please, no lamb." Her hand went over her mouth, and she closed her eyes.

"I thought you liked lamb?"

"Not today. Excuse me a minute, please." She stood and headed off to the bathroom.

What was that all about? Emily wasn't squeamish about food, I'd seen her eat things other people might not consider food, but the thought of lamb had made her sick. Maybe it was her medicine or a migraine coming on. Those sometimes made her stomach a little on the delicate side.

I hoped she wasn't coming down with something; now that we'd talked about Elmo's I really wanted to go. I ordered a glass of ginger ale for her when the waiter came to check on us and asked for some bread and butter to be brought to the table. Emily soon came back to the table, her complexion much better, and we ordered our dinner. I ordered steak, just to be on the safe side. I didn't want to bring on another bout of sickness if just the mention of lamb set her off.

"Do you want dessert?" I asked as our plates were taken away a short while later.

"I do," she said coyly, and I felt her foot against the inside of my calf beneath the table. "Just not from here."

She looked up, directly into my eyes, and I knew it wasn't food she was after. "Let's finish the night off right then, Emily."

I watched as satisfaction replaced the coyness in her eyes and quickly got us out of there. Before long, we were sitting in the bar area, watching Roxie do her stuff. The woman was talented, but I didn't need Roxie's seductive dance to get me in the mood. All I needed was Emily's whispers of how much she needed me.

It was fun to be out with her, though, and I couldn't lie, that new routine of Roxie's was hot. I watched her, unaware of just how riveted I was. Emily moved, but I couldn't look away. Another shuffle in the seat next to me, and I finally looked over at her. "What's up, pet?"

"Nothing, sir." She smiled at me, a cheeky expression on her face. She reached out to touch me, and I felt something soft and silky in her hand as it slid along my arm. I looked down and saw black satin.

"Getting adventurous are you, pet?" I knew she wanted me, and I wanted her just as much. The trick was to keep the tease alive.

"Maybe." She stood before she twisted down, her hips moving in slight circles. I looked up to see her hands twisting her hair around her head, her eyes seductive, before she bent forward, her eyes directly in front of mine.

I only had eyes for Emily then. She twisted close to me, and I felt her breasts slid against my face as she moved up. I scooted up in the seat, so that she was between my legs, and ran my hand up her skirt.

"Oh…" I heard her gasp as she let her head fall back, her hips twisting, as my fingers slid along her bare bottom.

The bar was full at that point, but most of the patrons were watching Roxie. Anyone could turn their head at any moment and see my hands up her skirt. "You know, if someone looks our way, Emily, they'll know exactly"—I paused and slid my right hand around her hip, then down to between her thighs—"where my hand is."

Her cheeks were flushed, and her eyes were riveted to mine. "Then let them watch, sir."

"Oh, indeed," I whispered and grinned up at her. She put her hands on my shoulders and straddled my thighs. Her hips continued to dance on me, and when my fingers slid into her, she gasped louder.

I heard more than a gasp when my thumb found her clit.

"Fuck." It left her lips softly, but I heard her. I heard the way she took in a deep breath to try to stay calm, to resist the pleasure I was giving. I hadn't told her she could come yet. She knew she had to wait. That was how it worked when we came in here. She didn't come until I told her to.

I pulled my hand away when Roxie's routine ended. I knew she'd spotted my precious little darling and would come to our table right away. I turned Emily around and pulled her to sit on my lap. She hummed when she felt my cock, hard and ready for her, nestled into her soft bottom. She pushed down on me slightly, just enough, with her back arched, just as Roxie made it to our table.

"Hey, I didn't know you two were coming tonight. How are you?" Roxie, an angel with blonde hair and blue eyes, leaned over to kiss Emily's cheek, and I swear, I did not groan at all. The thought of these two together had occurred to me before, but I'd kept it to myself. They didn't seem to hold an interest in each other that way, so it was one nice thought, but not something I'd ever act on or broach with Emily.

"Fine, honey, how are you?" I heard Emily ask, and gave a chin tilt to Roxie. Emily was shifting around on my dick, and fuck if it didn't feel good. She was doing it on purpose too. I could see it in the way her arms flexed and her back arched again.

"I'm good. I'm going to go and mingle, but it's good to see you. It's been a while." She bent down to kiss Emily again, and I groaned when Emily leaned forward to kiss her cheek. Quietly, though. I did have some control, after all.

After Roxie walked away, Emily and leaned back against me and turned so her mouth was right beside my ear. "Take me downstairs."

I didn't need to be told twice. I made to stand up, and she got off of me. I pulled her scarf off before we'd even made it to the elevator. By the time the door shut, I had her on my hips, her legs wrapped around my waist, as I kissed her deeply. She clung to me as if she was starving for my attention, and I fed her every ounce of it she wanted.

I wanted to open the zipper on my trousers and slide right into her, but I knew if I waited it would be so much better. Her hands were in my hair, tugging at the shorter strands, and I pulled my head away.

"I left enough for you to pull on." I licked her lips as she grinned and let her legs fall down. We were almost at the lower level.

"That's good. I was worried about that." Her lips moved along my jaw, and I could feel how hot my skin was.

Almost as hot as hers.

The elevator came to a stop and dinged.

She took my hand, leading me down the hall.

We passed a couple making love on a bed, their bodies entangled. The door was open, a clear invitation to watch. Emily passed that door and walked down further, Past the room with a woman on her knees as she serviced a woman chained to a wall. Further she went, past a variety of rooms, filled with a variety of sexual situations.

She kept going until she found a room that contained a man on a bed. He looked up at her as we passed, and Emily paused. She looked at him, then at me. I lifted my left eyebrow, and she nodded.

"As you wish, madam."

The man was handsome, his light red hair cut short and close to his head. He was naked, except for a pair of tight black boxer briefs. He smiled, tilted his head, and I saw the flash of green eyes. She liked the look of him, I guessed, and moved on to the room next to his. It was empty, and she left the lights off as we went in. She wanted to play the exhibitionist, and I wasn't about to stop her. It was her thing, and her night.

She went to the clear glass that separated the two rooms, and the man's head perked up. I sat on the bed, and we both watched my little angel as she slowly began to undress. He leaned back on his elbows at the edge of the bed, with his feet on the floor. His eyes were riveted to Emily as she began to pull her bra off.

For a moment, she hesitated and looked back at me.

"Have your fun, Emily. I love to see how much he wants you. How he wants to touch you but can't." I knew the man couldn't hear us, but he could see us. Just enough light spilled over from the other room to let him see us. "Go on, pet. Show him what he wants to see most."

She turned around and faced me, so he could see her bare ass. She'd already let the skirt fall to the floor, and the sweater was with it. Her eyes were on me as she unclasped the hooks of the bra. She held it to her chest for a moment, until she let that fall to the floor too.

"That's it, pet. Now turn around, and let him see you." Her eyes were intense, full of thoughts, and a whole lot of lust. We'd done similar things before, and I knew she wasn't bashful anymore. She was waiting for something more.

6

EMILY

I watched Dylan, fully clothed on the edge of the bed, and waited. I needed that signal, and when his eyes flicked behind me, I knew it was time. I turned around and looked up at the very tall man only inches away from me.

I tilted my head and met his gray eyes. His were hungry, avid to take me in. I let my head fall back and watched as his eyes drifted down my body. From the long, pale length of my neck, down to my breasts pressed into the glass, and down further.

I let my eyes travel down. He was paler than me, but that didn't detract from his looks. He was a handsome man, and he had a wonderful jawline, made for a lover's touch. Or their lips.

His hands came up to the glass, near my face. I didn't flinch away. I just waited to see what else he would do. I hadn't forgotten about Dylan, I never could, but I wanted to see how this man reacted to me. I'd only ever been with Dylan, but I had an exhibitionist streak I didn't know about. Not until I met Dylan, anyway.

The finger on the glass moved down, followed the path his eyes had taken, and I watched his face. His tongue darted out, wet his lips, and disappeared as his fingers traced down. They came to my breasts, and I saw hunger, deep hunger, as his palm flattened against the glass. I flicked a gaze back at Dylan, he shook his head in encouragement, and I moved closer and pressed my breasts into the glass.

I closed my eyes for a second, just a moment, and imagined his touch. Air sucked into my lungs as desire flared through me. I wanted his touch, but I liked knowing how much he wanted me even more. That was what it was about, about knowing someone else wanted me. That they wanted to touch me, fuck me, but couldn't.

I opened my eyes, full of my own momentary power, and looked up at him. I wondered if my eyes glowed with my pleasure, with my arrogance in that moment. I was the one in control, and we all knew it.

"Join me?" I asked Dylan with a slight turn of my head over my shoulder. I didn't take my eyes off of the man, however. I just waited, my eyes full of anticipation.

He moved away as Dylan came closer, and I had a

feeling I wouldn't be the one in control for long. At least not of my body.

"Move away from the glass, pet." His voice was thick, full of unsaid things and his need to control himself.

I leaned back into him, as he slid his hands around my waist, up my flat stomach, and to the pale breasts the stranger wanted to cup so much. I let my head fall back on Dylan's shoulder and watched the man.

He stepped out of his shorts and revealed his thick cock. It was shorter than Dylan's, but not too much. It made up for stature with girth, and I knew it would be just as fun to ride as Dylan's long, thick erection. He sat on the bed, his hands in his lap, but clasped together.

"Squeeze my nipples, Dylan." I knew he'd let me run the show for a little while. Maybe even the entire session, but he was a dominant male. So, maybe not.

For now, he did as I asked, and squeezed my nipples. The pressure was soft at first, but then it changed, became firmer, until I gasped. That was when he stopped, left the pressure alone, and just waited, his hard length pressed against my bottom.

The man's eyes narrowed, and I saw him breathe in a deep breath. I grinned at him then and slid my hand down, confident that he'd follow every move I made. His kink was to watch; of course he'd follow every move I made. When Dylan lifted my breasts as if he offered them to the man, something twisted inside of me, became warm and then hot. For now, I could forget all of my problems: the things I had to tell Dylan, and the things I had to decide on. For now, my life wasn't spiraling out of my control; it was on course and headed straight where I wanted it to go.

"He wants you so much, Emily. Look at the way his lips are parted, how hard he is for you." At Dylan's words I glanced down to the other man's dick, dark red and angry looking with his need.

"Then we best give him a show, Dylan." I turned into his arms and he backed us up to the bed. My hands were on his face as I followed him down, my legs straddled over his. We were on the side of the bed so that I could see the man and he could see me, and Dylan could watch us both.

"You like knowing he wants me, don't you, sir?" I asked, although I knew the answer. I needed to hear him say it. That was part of the game. I was the one in control, even though he had the power to stop this anytime he wanted to.

"I do, pet. I like knowing that he wants to fuck you until he can't fuck you anymore but can't. Because you are mine, Emily, and always will be."

Again, that something inside of me twisted and grew even hotter when Dylan said I would always be his. I leaned over and kissed him, became lost in his hot flesh and his wet kiss. I felt him between my thighs, so ready for me, and I pushed myself up.

I turned my head to the right to look at the man as I sank down onto Dylan's cock, and I bit my lip provocatively. It felt so good to sink down onto the man I loved while in the next room, removed but so involved, stood a man who wanted to see me come. The thought of it all made me shiver as I began to move on Dylan.

I was in control, completely in control, with his hands on my hips no more than an anchor. I started slow and built us up, but kept an eye on both men. The man next door was close, yet he hadn't even touched himself, but I wanted him to wait, to join us in that moment. I held his eyes and urged him to take the next step, to follow the pace I'd set.

It wasn't long before his hand fluttered down, over the flat plane of his stomach, and further down, until he took himself in hand.

Within seconds of his surrender to my will, I slid my hand down to find the part of me that pulsed with a deep ache. My fingers sank into wet desire, and all of my pleasure became focused on that one single point. I shivered in a breath of air, my eyes still pinned to the stranger's next door.

His head tilted back as he watched me, as if he wanted to tempt me to him. I had what I wanted between my thighs already. I sank a hand onto Dylan's thigh behind me and bounced a little deeper, a little harder, my thighs clamped to his hips.

"You trying to make him come, Emily? Because that's what's going to happen if you keep looking at him like that. Like you're daring him to break the rules and come to fuck you. He can barely control himself. Look how hard he's gritting his teeth."

I broke eye contact long enough to look into Dylan's eyes. He was grinning, that arrogant grin that told me he knew he was still in control. I sank down deeper and squeezed him from the inside, just to remind him we shared control.

"I know what I'm doing," I said and bent forward to kiss him. Dylan surprised me. He flipped me over and moved us until my head was pointed at the man. I had to crane my neck back to see him, but I could. "No fair!"

"I think he needs to know who's really in control here, pet; otherwise, we might have a problem on our hands that I'm not sure you're ready for yet."

I stared into the man's eyes, unwilling to let go just yet. I needed to see his ecstasy. I needed to watch him let go.

Then Dylan was inside of me again, over me, and I lost myself in him. The man would have to fend for himself. I had far more to contend with than he could offer me. I licked the sweat from his neck and bit down as he fucked into me hard and fast. I heard him groan above me and knew he was close.

I wrapped myself around him, my hand between us, as he began to speak again.

"He craves you now, Emily, the way I crave you. He won't be able to get you out of his head. He'll think about you when he comes now; he'll think about you the next time he comes. Just like I do."

I felt that first warning signal that the world was about to shatter and pressed harder into my clit with a finger that made tight circles in the wet skin.

"He'll want you, Emily, he'll want to fuck you. He will never, ever touch you."

I gasped as he paused to thrust deeper, into just the right spot, and the world began to spin away now. I felt that liquid pulse, and I cried out Dylan's name.

"That's right, pet. You're mine, and that's why he can look, but he will never be able to touch you. You're mine."

I threw my head back, my eyes blurring, but for a moment, I saw the man's face, twisted in pleasure, one hand on the glass to brace his body as he followed me into bliss. And then Dylan joined us, and I followed all over again. I would follow Dylan to the end of the earth.

"YOU KNOW, you still haven't come to a conclusion about what you're going to do, Emily."

I tensed because it hadn't been my brother that was on my mind, but the baby. It was still so new and very weird to think about. We were home now, in bed, the lights off as we both attempted to get to sleep. My thoughts were keeping me awake, and it would seem Dylan's were keeping him up.

"I guess I should agree to see him, shouldn't I?" I held my breath and waited for his answer. I was facing away from him, on the edge of the bed, curled into a ball.

"That's up to you, darling." He sighed and rolled over to me. He didn't pull me to face him, or move me in any way; he just curled around me, and that might have been the best hug he'd ever given me. He was there for me, and he would accept whatever I decided, that hug told me. His left arm was under his head, but his right wrapped around my stomach, and I tensed all over again.

I had to tell him about the baby, a baby he'd helped create. He had a right to know, and he would. Just as soon as I faced my fear. I also had this other matter to deal with, and right now, it looked as if I had far more time to deal with the baby situation than I did the family situation.

Which only reminded me of how much I wanted to talk to Jessi.

"I really miss my sister-in-law, Jessi. She was my best friend throughout our lives. Things changed when she married my brother, and I can't be mad at her for that. Marriage changes you, and babies change you even more. Well, changes your priorities anyway."

I let the sentence hang, mainly because I realized what I'd just said. I'd been so upset with her for forgetting me, but that was my problem. She'd moved on with her life, and I couldn't blame her for that. I had my own little bun in the oven to prove how much a baby could change your life. I'd only just found out about mine, and already the world had changed.

The true impact, and all of the things that would change, hadn't truly occurred to me yet, but they were starting to dawn on me. I was about to bring another human being into the world, and I was excited about that, but the rest, I dreaded. The hardest part would be telling Dylan that he was going to be a father. That kept me quiet for a long time. How was I supposed to break this to him?

Scenarios played out in my head. Cute little ways to reveal the fact seemed to be for families, married couples, or people who had been together far longer than we'd been. For people not on birth control. I couldn't even remember how far along the doctor said I was, it was that much of a shock.

It might only be two weeks, or it could have been

more. I knew that baby must have been determined to be born, though. It hadn't been long since I'd missed my shot, and I'd only been on the migraine medicine for a short while. I'd read in the literature I'd been given that it could take a woman six months to get pregnant after the shot wore off.

Which was another reason I hadn't been too worried about the whole situation. Of course, it wasn't the most responsible thing in the world to have forgotten to get my shot renewed, but I was new to all of this. I'd thought I was being so grownup when I got the shot, and then I read all the material like an adult should; then, I'd gone and fucked up on my very first round.

I knew pills like antibiotics could make the birth control fail, but I hadn't realized there were so many others that could do it. Now, I couldn't sleep because I had to figure out how in the world I was going to tell Dylan.

Which was all the more reason to connect with the family, wasn't it? I could get advice from my sisters-in-law about this. They'd all married my brothers, and that had taken some courage, in my opinion. Not a one of them were easy to get along with, and each one had their foibles. Obviously, in the case of Trent.

I thought it would take an awfully long time to forgive and forget in his case. The rest? Well, they'd driven me away without even realizing it. Maybe I'd been a little bit unfair to them. I breathed out completely, my head a mess and my heart hurting.

I put my hand over Dylan's arm, flat across my stomach. I knew the man I'd met, so determined to make me get on my knees and submit to him, had become someone else since that night. He wasn't so desperate for control now, he didn't seem as … lost. He knew what he wanted, he always had, even back then.

I didn't think he'd quite counted on what he wanted changing into something he'd never experienced before. I scoffed softly at that thought. It pleased me to know that I'd tamed my raging bull. A little bit, at least. I didn't want him to be a different man, not at all. I'd been attracted to that wild, yet controlled, man he'd been when I'd first met him.

I loved him, and I thought I knew him well enough now to know that he would probably accept what had happened and deal with it, but then again, it might be what would tip him over the edge. It wasn't that I feared being alone through this; I'd face raising my child alone if it came down to it.

It would be shattering the relationship that Dylan and I had that would break me. If he thought I'd done this on purpose and ended our relationship, he'd be ending his own chance at a life he was only starting to realize he'd wanted. Well, not all men wanted children, but I had a feeling Dylan would come around to the idea. After all, he hadn't wanted our relationship, and look where we were now.

If he did end the relationship, though, I would mourn for what he'd lost more than what I'd lose. I might be able to give love another chance one day, maybe, but him? He'd hide in his rooftop penthouse and would never attempt it again. So this was far more than just 'oops, I'm pregnant, baby'. This was 'we might have fucked up in a huge way'.

I kept picturing that little boy he used to be, alone after the fire was put out, being driven away in a stranger's car. That little boy deserved love back then, and the grown man deserved it now. In the end, it would be up to him to decide what he wanted more—a future where he was protected from life's fuck ups, or one where we got to enjoy them together.

7

DYLAN

I stared at the row of medicine on my desk and thought about the fact that I still hadn't told Emily what was wrong with me. I'd meant to, but the right time just never seemed to crop up. It wasn't something you could simply drop on purpose, was it?

Hi, Emily. I know we've just moved in together, and I know this is a huge step for both of us, but, well, I might soon become very ill. The kind that might require medical care and a lot of time in bed. Not in that way we are used too. The kind that might kill me.

My gut clenched on that last thought, and I grabbed the pills to pop them in my mouth. I swallowed them with a bottle of orange juice and swept the bottles into my desk. Emily never came in here, so I kept them in there, hidden away.

My phone chirped, as if she knew I was thinking

about her, and I saw a text from her. She wanted to know if it was alright if she met with her brother's wife. Of course, it was, these people were her family.

Although, I had told her time and time again that she should give the reunion a try. I wouldn't trust Trent Thompson as far as I could throw him, but he was her brother. She was from a large family and knew how integral they were in her life. I had come from a tiny family; even after my adoption, there'd only been three of us. Emily's family was huge in comparison, and with the children her brothers had spawned there were a lot more Thompsons to go around. She deserved to be a part of that. Even if I did think Trent was an asshole.

She'd told me she'd cut them out of her life because they'd come to take her for granted. I could understand her reasoning, but Trent had taken it too far. He'd disowned her when she'd started a relationship with me. That simply wasn't fair, and I might be many things, but unfair wasn't one of them. I tapped at icons until the phone began to call Emily.

"Hi, baby." I heard her purr down the line and smile. She wasn't too upset then.

"Hiya, Emily. Listen, why don't you invite your sister-in-law to lunch, and I'll fend for myself. It's a baby step. She's family through marriage alone, and she can help you test the waters."

"I'm afraid, Dylan. I just don't want to get sucked back into their bullshit, you know?"

"So stand your ground, darling. Tell them to back off when they overstep their bounds. Walk away if they can't respect that. Show them that you aren't to be trifled with."

"That can be easier said than done." I heard her sigh and frowned.

"Emily, you had me in a room, your toy for a good hour, as you let another man watch me fuck you. If you can manage that, you can manage your family. Just face them with that same resolve, my dear. You'll have them eating out of your palm."

The urge to tell her I loved her suddenly overwhelmed me, and I had to blink a few times. I wasn't sure where that came from, but as she vacillated on the other end of the line, I knew I did. I knew I cared about her, thought I might love her, but it suddenly became profoundly clear that I did love this woman.

"You can rest easy knowing that if any of them break your heart, baby, I will break their face. Or ruin them, whichever comes first."

"Oh, don't be violent, Dylan," she started, but I chuckled, and she knew I wasn't too serious. Only a little. "I know you'll be there for me. Otherwise, I'd burn the letter and get on with my life."

"Good. Now make your plans; I have work to do,"

she agreed and hung up. I sat at the desk, stunned at myself.

I was in love, for the very first time in my life. Completely in love. Not a little bit, a whole lot. I frowned. Was it fair to Emily, this love of mine? She'd obviously come to rely on me as a partner, a confidant, and respected my opinion when it came to her decisions. The problem I had was I'd failed to be upfront with her about my health. It wasn't something she could catch from me, but it would impact our quality of life.

Perhaps I'd been a bit delusional asking her to move in with me. It would make it harder to keep from her, if I didn't soon tell her. Fuck, so many things suddenly occurred to me that I kind of felt like an idiot. Things that should have been clear the moment I'd asked her for that second contract.

I should have walked away. I should have left her to her life. She would have found someone who could love her and give her the guarantee of a future. Instead, I'd been selfish. I'd wanted her with me. I'd wanted her.

Now I had her, for however long that might be. I didn't think she'd abandon me once she found out what was wrong; Emily wasn't that kind of person. She would stick by me and do whatever it took to help me. I didn't want her to do that alone.

Which was what had really made my stomach twist into a knot. I wouldn't be able to let her go, not now that she was so important to me. And at some point, she'd need support from someone who wasn't me, because she'd be taking care of me. She needed her family, and it didn't matter how much I might hate Trent for the way he'd treated us both; he was her brother.

That meant I had to hide my animosity behind a smile and fake it for her. I could do that, I decided. I could do whatever it took to make sure Emily would be taken care of, if there would come a day when I couldn't do it.

It wasn't quite what I'd expected to happen when I came to Myrtle Beach to look for a place to set up here. I'd planned to go back to Kansas and then maybe to wander around the west coast until it was time to focus on this place. All of that had changed when I met Emily. She'd changed a lot of things for me.

"Hey, you want to come down and see me for a bit, before you wander off for the day?" I texted to her. As expected, it took only seconds to get a response.

"On my way." She'd even put in a smiley face emoji.

A few minutes later she was opening my door, a big smile on her face. She had on a pair of faded jeans that fit her snugly, a dark blue tank top that fanned out around her hips, and a pair of sandals. She was ready for a casual lunch and not a day at work. Which was fine, she could do as she pleased and wear whatever she liked, whether at work or not.

"You look lovely," I said as she came to sit in my lap. I brushed an ash blonde streak of hair out of her eyes and kissed her chin. "How are you?"

"I'm not too bad. Why did you want to see me?" Her lips were tracing up to my ear from my chin, and her hot breath on my neck was doing things I didn't have time to act on.

I could make time.

"I just wanted to see you; do I have to have a reason?" I looked up into her eyes, gray like mine, but so different. Hers sparkled with silver and were a lighter color than mine.

"No, I suppose not." She wrapped her arms around my neck and snuggled in, my hands on her waist to keep her in place.

"Are you going to meet your sister-in-law?" I prodded, as she didn't volunteer the information.

"No, I have reservations made at one of my favorite places with Roxie in a couple of hours. I was about to cancel but changed my mind. I'll ask Jessi to meet me there in a couple of days. At least if the lunch doesn't go well, I can have some good food."

"Why wouldn't it go well?"

"I don't know. Jessi might try to brush it all away and not see my side of things. She might take Trent's side..."

"Is it fair to make her take sides?" It was only a question, not an indictment, and she pondered it quietly before she responded.

"Maybe not, but I refuse to go into this without knowing where I stand. If it's going to end up the same way in a few months, or if they expect me to just become their nanny again, what's the point? I want them all to know that."

"You have a job now, and a relationship; you can't be at their beck and call anyway."

"No, that privilege is reserved for you now." She kissed the tip of my nose and grinned at me. "You're right. I have things to do, and they have to respect that. Which is my point; they have to respect me this time, or I'll walk away for good. Only this time, I won't think twice about throwing away any letters that might come my way."

"Good girl, stand your ground." I kissed her forehead and pulled her face up to kiss her. "I hope it all works out for you, darling. You deserve to have as much love as you can get, you know?"

I heard her breath hitch in her throat, and she looked away. Was that hurt in her eyes, or just confusion?

"Emily? What's wrong? What did I say?" I pulled her face back to mine and looked at her closely.

"Nothing." She swiped at a tear and smiled a wobbly smile. "Sometimes, you are the sweetest man in the world, do you know that?"

"No, I'm not." I chuckled but meant it. "I don't think I'm sweet at all, but you'd know more about that than me."

"You are. You deserve some love too, you know?" She wouldn't look at me at first, but then she did.

Her eyes were clear, without any sadness. "Do I?"

I wasn't sure why I asked the question, but I was curious to know her answer.

"Of course, you do, Dylan. We all do. You're not a monster. You might need a dozen people to kiss your ass and tell you how wonderful you are, but you do deserve to be loved. By at least one person."

"I see." I didn't want to ask her, but I could see it in her eyes.

Was it possible she loved me as much as I loved her?

"Good. Do you want me to bring you something back for lunch?" She let it all go, just like that, and didn't push.

She knew the relationship we had was unconventional, but she didn't complain about it. She accepted it and didn't push for more. Which was one of the reasons I loved her. She'd given me time to.

"No, I'll find something at home. You go and enjoy yourself. Don't worry about me." I let the moment go, the same way she did, but I knew it wouldn't be long before we both circled back to it. It was inevitable by now.

8

EMILY

"It's all changed, I take it?" Roxie's bright blue eyes flashed at me across the table and I wanted to scowl at her. Mainly, because she was right.

"You know it has." I sighed out and was glad the waiter had taken our orders already. It would be a while before he came back.

"Is it bad? Do you need a place to crash?" Roxie's eyes were filled with concern and just a hint of a menace. "Do I need to pick up my baseball bat?"

"Oh, not at all!" I leaned over and hissed at her. "It's not Dylan. It's my … erm, brother."

I looked down at my hands on the table and knew that wasn't the only problem. The baby was the main problem. I'd been queasy that morning, but it had passed after an hour or so. I was glad to know why I was sick now, but at the same time, the baby made me anxious.

"Hmm. Let me have a look at you." I saw her squinting at me and suspected she was checking me for bruises. She looked me over, far more thoroughly than she had when we met in the parking lot, and nodded. "I see."

"You see what, exactly? A woman whose family is insane? A woman with the man of her dreams waiting on her at home, only she has this weird family that won't leave her alone and keeps fucking things up?"

"Something like that." If I could ever describe a smile as knowing, it would be the one Roxie had on right now.

"What, are you a fortune teller now?" I grinned to ease the tension I felt in my jaw.

"Maybe. How's Dylan?" The change of subject made me blink, but I answered her.

"He's fine. Incredible. Generous. Loving even. Can you believe that? Loving?" I shook my head, confounded. "It's amazing."

"Sometimes, all a man needs is a little bit of love to change him. That loosens them right up." I heard a country twang in her voice but didn't comment. She was Southern, and you knew it the minute she spoke, but every now and then her voice took on this edge that screamed country girl.

I guessed she'd practiced some to lose that, but I wasn't about to judge her. My parents paid for elocution lessons to make sure I didn't sound like a bumpkin. It wasn't any different, really.

"I would agree in his case. He's just, well, different, you know?"

"I thought you two would be a good match." I saw a hint of sadness in her eyes, but then it disappeared. "I almost took him myself, but … well, I was claimed at that point, so you're a lucky girl, Emily."

"I didn't know that. What did you like about him?" I was curious, not jealous. Roxie wasn't the kind to try to steal a man from a friend.

"Oh, you know how he comes across all cocky and arrogant? That cold, hard gaze of his, and the way he kind of barks at people? Well, I saw right through that, to the man who just needed some loving in his life. I'm afraid we're too alike, Dylan and I, so we'd have probably broken each other anyway. It's better he got you instead. You're the better woman." She patted my hand and leaned back, satisfied.

"I doubt that, Roxie, my parents just happened to be rich. I'm no different, otherwise."

"You are, Emily, and it's not just that money you were born into. You're good, from the bottom up. I've not always been the best person in the world. I'm happy with who I am now, though. It took me a while, but I got there."

"I like you just how you are, Roxie. My adventurous, no-nonsense, no-bullshit friend."

"Good, 'cause I ain't a-changin' for nobody." She put the accent on thick this time, but it came with a grin, so I knew she was teasing me.

"Lord, you're going to be the death of me, woman." I laughed and put my own accent on.

The waiter came over, and I saw how he checked Roxie out. She had on a pair of slouchy black pants, and a loose black silk tank top, with a pair of black sandals on her feet. She looked casual, but still had that something that oozed sexiness. Men often looked at her like that, but she never seemed to notice.

I guessed when people always looked at you like that you stopped taking notice of it after a while. She smiled at me, her makeup perfect and not too much, just perfect for her complexion and looks. She really was a beautiful woman, and I hated that her last companion had dumped her. She didn't seem to mind being alone, though.

"How are things at work?" The waiter had brought our salads and left, a pink tinge in his cheeks when she thanked him with a tap on the hand.

He must be in his twenties, but he'd blushed like a teenaged boy when she touched him. I smothered a laugh and tipped my salad dressing over the pile of lettuce, chicken, and parmesan cheese in my bowl.

"It's alright. I'm going down to Jacksonville tomorrow. I have a competition down there, then I'll be back up the next day." She knew I liked to hear about her dancing competitions. She was one of the best exotic dancers around, and she had the titles to prove it.

"I wish I could go and watch you." I stuck a bite of chicken in my mouth and wondered if it was possible. I had work to do, though, and I needed to take the job seriously if I expected the staff to treat me with respect.

"I'll have another one at some point, don't worry. I'm glad to hear you have a job with Dylan. That's important. How do you like it?"

"I like it so far. I'm doing a little bit of everything until he gets all of the staff hired. After that, I'll have less to do. Or more, I guess. The resort will be open then."

"I hope it stays enjoyable, at least." She tucked into her own salad, and then our main courses came soon after.

Before I knew it, I was in my car and driving back to the resort. I went up to the penthouse to change and saw that Dylan had left me a note.

"Hope your lunch was fun, I'll see you this evening." He'd scrawled his name underneath, and I grinned as I held the note to my heart.

He was always doing this, leaving me notes around the place. It was sweet and he didn't know it, but I tucked them all into my underwear drawer, as if they were love notes. Sometimes he wrote the notes on a receipt, sometimes a bit of torn paper, but to me they might as well have been written on vellum with gold ink, because I treasured each one.

I changed quickly and put on a pair of black pants, a black silk t-shirt, and a pair of black heels. They were my favorite Louboutin's, a pair of black patent leather stilettos. I stared down at them, and not for the first time that day, thought about how much being pregnant would change my life.

I wasn't always the most balanced woman in the world, and a fall could be dangerous. The words *in my condition* played through my mind, and I smiled, such old-fashioned words. The shoes were impractical, however, and I put them back and reached for a pair of black Versace ballerina slippers. Also, black patent leather with a gold embellishment across the toe. Much more sensible and safer.

Which made me think. I might not carry the baby to term. It was an odd though that came out of nowhere, but it made me sit up. What if I told Dylan I was pregnant, he broke up with me, and then I lost the baby? A cold thought, but logical. I'd have wrecked our relationship over a child that didn't happen.

Maybe I should wait to tell him, until I knew I was past the three-month mark, at least? Then, I could tell him, and we'd go from there. I could wait the entire nine months, just disappear and come back with a baby in my arms, if I wanted to get carried away with it, but that would just be stupid. No, I'd wait until the three-month mark, then I'd tell him.

With my decision made, I stood up, shook out the loose tank top, and headed for the door. I had work to get done. I made my way down to the elevator, happy now that I'd made a decision. Come what may, I'd tell him about the baby.

I met with some of the new staff, the chef Dylan had hired, and the general manager of the restaurant. Then, I met the new housekeeping brigade and made sure they had what they needed to get ready the grand opening. I went over some order forms that the staff at the pool had sent in by email and sent that on to Dylan. They all knew I was Dylan's live-in girlfriend, and I was worried it would be hard to get them to take me seriously, but everybody had so far, and I hadn't had any problems.

It was nice to be taken seriously and to have some say in things. I'd done a lot for my family and had often filled empty roles for the family's resorts all over the world, but I'd always been my father's daughter. To be obeyed, but never taken seriously. No major decisions had ever been left up to me, and if I ever received calls about them it was to find out where my father or Trent was.

Now, people actually valued my opinion, and that

was something else I had to thank Dylan for. I was part of a team and important. I guessed to most people it would be silly to think like that, but to me, well, it was really nice.

"Are you free, madam?" I heard Dylan sing out as he came into my office.

"I'm free, Dylan." It was a line from a very old British television show that we'd found one night, during a binge of British shows on YouTube we'd come across. We both loved the show, and the line, and we found ourselves saying it at times.

"I've ordered dinner from the chef, kind of his first test." Dylan wiggled his eyebrows at me in a comic manner, and I snorted at him. "I've got a selection of very bad horror films chosen for your perusal, and then a rather good fucking planned, if you should so desire, madam."

"Oh, that sounds like my kind of night." I giggled as he kicked the door closed and came over to lean over me for a kiss. "That sounds like a rather magical night, in fact."

"I thought so. I wouldn't want to disappoint, madam." His lips nuzzled up my neck to behind my ear, and I tilted my head as he did so. "I know how you love really bad horror films, after all."

"Ah, I thought it was the rather good fucking that you thought wouldn't disappoint me." I pulled back to look in his glittering eyes and twisted my lips in mock disapproval. "You aren't teasing me now, are you?"

"As if I'd tease about such a thing." He knelt in front of me and let his hands skim up my parted thighs. "In fact, it's a shame you put pants on, Emily."

"The door does lock, Dylan," I offered, hopeful.

"I know," he rocked back onto his heels and tapped at his chin. "I was hoping to push it up around your waist while I buried my face in you."

"Oh my." My eyes were round, and I had to shift around in my seat. "I can go change, if you'd like?"

"No,"—he tapped at his chin again, his eyes scrunched up—"that might ruin the mood. Better to just strip these off of you, I guess."

He wasted no time in getting the pants off of me, or his face between my thighs. I propped my feet on my desk and used it as leverage to push my hips against him. His tongue teased me, hot and knowing, as I gave myself up to his attention. There weren't many people who would come into my office, and I hoped if someone came to my door, they'd knock first.

The thrill that we could be caught heightened the moment, and I kept glancing at the door. I didn't want it to open, but knowing it could made this all the more clandestine. Dylan owned the place, it wasn't like we'd be fired if we were caught, but knowing the danger was there was nice.

"Dylan," I sighed as my fingers tangled in his hair. "You do that so well."

"Mmm." The vibration of the sound against me was sensational.

In a matter of seconds my back arched, and I was trying not to scream his name. He was an expert in making me come and knew how to get me off quickly by now. Sometimes, he'd make me wait, make me beg for release, but now wasn't one of those times. I was glad about that, because a knock came at the door just as I put my pants on and sat down.

I was disappointed because I'd wanted to return the favor.

"I'm sorry, Dylan." I looked up at him, regret in my eyes.

"Don't worry, darling, you can make it up to me later. On your knees." He kissed me and walked out of the office and left the door open.

"I'm sorry, I didn't mean to interrupt." It was the head of groundskeeping. He looked nervous but soon calmed down.

"What can I do for you?" I asked and settled into my seat.

"Well, we need a few more temporary staff to finish getting the new plants in on time, and the front desk sent me to you."

"Ah, no problem, we'll get it sorted out." I made a

phone call and sent him down to the right person for that.

It was nice, even if all I could do was make a phone call.

I knew that wasn't the reason for my smile, though. That was all Dylan's doing. He seemed to have this sixth sense about when I needed reminding that I had something to smile about. There was one thing for sure, Dylan James was an expert at leaving me with a smile.

9

DYLAN

"I'm not so sure this is a good idea, Dylan." Her voice was quiet, almost imperceptible, but I heard her.

"You know I can turn this car around and take you home; just say the words, Emily." I meant it too, whatever she wanted was what I would do.

She'd decided to meet up with her entire family, to give them a chance, after she'd thought about it for a few more days. She had initially just wanted to meet up with her sister-in-law, but then she'd decided it was a Band-Aid situation. Rip it off and get it over with, which was how she usually faced things.

She was brave, my woman, and it made me proud of her. If she wanted to turn around and leave, that was just as brave to me. Either way, it was Emily's decision, and she would make up her mind. That was what was important. I'd also make sure her family stuck to that decision and didn't bother her.

They'd really hurt her over the years, and I didn't think they knew exactly how they'd abused their relationship with her. From what she'd said she was just a token member, and I wasn't certain if that was because she was female, because she'd been born last, or if it was something about her that they just didn't appreciate. I thought she was the goddess I'd spent a long time looking for, without knowing I was, I thought with a smirk.

"What do you want to do?" I slowed the car on a quiet residential street and pulled over. I looked at her and saw nervousness mixed with doubt.

"I should do this, right?" Her lips trembled, and she all but vibrated with indecision.

"Emily, try it, my dear. See what happens. If they piss you off or say something that upsets you, we'll leave, and that will be the end of it." I put my hand over hers, and I could actually feel calm go through her.

I felt a swell in my chest at her reaction, and a sense of pride I didn't know it was possible to feel. I'd given her comfort, and that made me happy.

"Alright. We can do this. Slay the dragon, right?" Her eyes were shining with confidence now, instead of fear, and I shook my head.

"I wouldn't call Trent a dragon, a dick maybe, but not

a dragon. Aren't dragons supposed to be sexy in all those romance novels women leave in the rooms of the resorts now?"

"I guess. I've seen a few of those. They look … interesting." I saw a smirk cross her face this time and grinned outright. I'd taught the woman to smirk, fuck yeah.

I loved it when she got that dirty look on her face, in whatever situation, a cross between elven and cocky; it was a knockout look.

"Mmhmm. I bet." I put the car in drive and followed her directions to her brother's house.

She'd told them I was coming and refused to come if I wasn't welcomed. She'd made that clear, both of us or neither of us, that was the deal. I was really creating a monster, it would seem, but I didn't care. She was my monster.

I pulled into the driveway, clasped her hand one more time, looked into her eyes and waited for her to nod. She did, so I got out of the car, and she joined me as I made it to the front. "Let's do this, Emily."

"Yes, sir." She winked at me, and I knew it would be okay. For the next minute or so anyway.

The door opened before we'd even made it to the steps, and children flew out of the empty space. Two twin little girls, no more than five-years-old, wrapped their arms around Emily's hips and screamed with joy.

"Aunt Emily! Where have you been?" one asked, her eyes tilted up to Emily's.

"I've been a little busy, my love, how are you, Breanna?" I wasn't sure how she could tell them apart.

They looked exactly alike and were dressed in the same outfits. I stared at them, totally stumped about which one was which and how I'd ever tell them apart.

"I've missed you terribly, Aunt Emily. I cried! Where were you?" the other one asked, and Emily knelt down on the concrete path that led to the steps.

"I'm so sorry, Rhiannon. I didn't want you to cry." She wrapped her arms around both girls, and I saw how she struggled to swallow down tears. This was what she'd missed, and it hit me hard.

She'd been denied even this little bit of love, which right now, looked like more love than one person could ever ask for. Trent's hatefulness had done this. Emily hadn't denied these girls anything, her brother had. I swallowed down my emotions, pushed the anger down, so that I could get through this with Emily without punching anyone.

"Come on, girls, let's go see the rest of the family," Emily said, and we all looked up to the house.

A woman stood there, rather pretty, with a nervous smile on her slim face. She had dark brown hair, hazel eyes, and was around Emily's height. Her smile wobbled for a second, and then she held her arms out to Emily.

She pulled Emily tight to her, and I heard quiet sobs from both.

I looked around, useless at that moment, and tried not to make myself conspicuous. I felt a tug on the jacket of my suit and looked down at a face so much like Emily's only smaller. The little girl even had Emily's gray eyes.

"Who are you, mister?" she asked, and her sister immediately piped up.

"He's her *boyfrien'*, silly." The little voice that dropped the 'd' in boyfriend, dripped sarcasm in a quiet whisper at her sister, and I could see that although Emily might not be their mother, she had influenced them. I couldn't help but smile at it all.

"Your sister's right. I'm Emily's boyfriend." I didn't want to say a name because I had no clue which was which.

I took a deep breath and realized that was the first time I'd said that to anyone. I was someone's boyfriend, or boyfrien' as the little girl had called me. It was all weird, but I was surprised to find I didn't mind. I'd never had a family, but already it was living up to my expectations of what having a large family would mean.

Before I knew it, I'd been introduced to seven children, two of which were babies, three wives, Emily's mother and father, and to Trent. The one who had kicked her out of this group full of so much love. Each wife and brother, niece and nephew had a moment alone with Emily, and even her parents took her aside.

Her eyes were red, and her nose looked raw from all of the crying, but she was happy. Very happy. I could see it in the way her shoulders relaxed and how much she laughed. Emily didn't laugh just to appease someone or fill quiet. She laughed only when she meant it.

Then I met the group of people spread around the house. Her brothers Kevin and Mason sized me up in the kitchen when I went in to find Emily some juice. They stared at me, silent, and I stared back. Then Kevin had grinned, and both held out their hands to me.

"Great to meet you, I'm Kevin."

"I'm Mason, the better-looking one. How are ya?"

Two sets of hands were shook, and I introduced myself, although it had nonchalantly been done already.

"I'm good. Big family, huh?" I raised my eyebrows and stuck my hands in my pockets.

"Yeah, it gets noisy sometimes, but it's nice." Kevin grinned and stuck a baby bottle in a bottle warmer. "Babies are great too, by the way. Never thought I'd say it, but there ya go."

"You're Bridget's dad?" I asked, not totally sure which child belonged to which parent yet.

"Yeah, and soon to be uncle to this one's upcoming addition. Which is why he's on bottle duty for Jessi." He laughed as he mentioned his sister-in-law's name.

"Get some practice in, huh?" It was an odd conversation, but it was conversation.

"That's the idea." Mason grinned, and Kevin laughed.

"Who knew we'd end up like this?" Mason looked up at me and shook his head. "The word daddy was not in my vocabulary, and now we're expecting our first child. It's a miracle after Laura's battle with cancer."

I smiled to hide the pain the words caused. It confused me why it caused me pain, but it did. Was it because I might never be able to have a child of my own? I'd never really thought about it, but now that I knew I might not live to see a child grow up, I had to wonder if it was fair. What about the medicine I was on? Would that cause problems?

I turned around and rummaged in the fridge until I found a bottle of juice for Emily. I didn't want them to see my face. I had to take a deep breath to get rid of the thoughts, to get rid of the pain, and focus on what was important.

"Well, good luck with the new baby," I said to Mason and left the kitchen.

I met Trent in the hallway of the large house and looked him straight in the eye.

"Look, I was dick." He swiped a hand over his mouth and looked away before he pinned those gray eyes so like Emily's on me. It was a family trait then.

It was a little disconcerting, but I was getting used to it now. Time to focus on what the man had to say.

"I can never make it up to Emily, what I did to her, but I can say I'm sorry to you, Dylan. I've talked with her, and well, I did you wrong, man. Sorry about that. Can we be friends, for my sister's sake?"

His eyes said he'd punch me if I didn't agree, and that was good with me. I was there for Emily, and for once the man seemed to be thinking of her too. That was real good.

"No worries, Trent. Emily's all that matters in this. I'm glad you reached out to her." I didn't want to rub it in his face that he'd caved, but I wanted him to know he had caused all of this. To be fair, he'd just admitted as much.

"I am too. It was Jessi who finally knocked some sense into me. My wife is something else, I got to tell you." He shook his head ruefully and smiled. "She's great. You taking that to Emily?"

He pointed at the juice, and I nodded. "Yeah, let me get this to her. Great talking to you."

I liked that we didn't have to go over everything for an hour, just a few sentences and the bridges that had been burned were suddenly replaced with new ones. Good. Emily deserved some peace, after the time she had. She might need this love if, when, my illness finally took hold.

Hopefully, that would be a long time from now, but there was no guarantee. It was possible she might end up on her own, and I knew, from the love her family had finally realized she needed, that she would be taken care of. She might not be okay if something happened to me, but she would be taken care of.

Suddenly, my arms were filled with warm, wiggly baby goodness, and I stared down into its little eyes. They were wise eyes, curious, and his little tongue curled around his open mouth before he grinned up at me. I assumed it was a boy anyway; the baby was dressed in blue.

"Can you please take him for a second? I need the bathroom so bad," Jessi rushed by me, her perfume the only hint that she'd only been there a second ago.

I stood there, trying to make sure the little guy didn't wiggle out of my arms. I was certain I would drop him, so I sank down in the now empty hallway and held him close to my chest. "Don't you dare fall, little guy. I'll never live it down. I'm sure your aunty would scream at me too."

He just wiggled his head around and grinned again. I decided it wasn't so bad. He smelled clean, what people called baby smell. Lotion and soap, I guessed, I didn't know; I'd heard it in passing somewhere along the way.

It was one of those profound moments that you don't know is happening until after. I was a grown man, yet, I'd never held a baby. A tiny little person who was totally helpless and needed love and nurturing from the grownups around him. He was … awesome.

"What are you doing in the hallway, Dylan?" I heard Emily's voice and looked up. She glanced down and saw the baby in my arms.

"You've got Harry, I see." She had this smile on her face, one that was filled with wonder. "You look. Um. Wow, you're good at that. He's actually smiling."

She sank down beside me, her black leggings and loose blue silk shirt a softness at my side. She didn't take the baby, or even offer to take him. She just watched.

I wanted to say, don't go getting ideas, because I could see it on her face that she was, but something stopped me. Would it be so bad, having something as incredible as this in our lives? I looked at her and could feel how wide my eyes were.

Fucking hell, have I gone over the edge that far for this woman? I gazed into her eyes and knew I might have.

I held the baby and watched him, Emily silent beside me, until his mother came back and took him from me. Little Harry was gone, and so was his tiny little warmth and that heavy but light sensation I'd felt with him in my arms. I sat there for a moment and just took it in.

"You okay?" Emily asked, and I looked at her.

"Of course. Just thinking. You have a bigger family

than I realized." I took her hand, and we stood up together.

"Is it scary?"

"No, just a surprise that's all." I looked around at the women and men gathered in the room, little ones who were old enough in the floor playing. It wasn't anything like I'd expected at all.

I'd expected immaculate coldness and quiet children who sat in chairs against the wall as the grownups spoke. The idea of a rich family that showed up in so many. Impersonal, uncaring, cold. Not this warmth and sprawl that ignored messy pillows on the couch and a spill of crayons all over the floor.

I think I might grow to like this.

DYLAN

 still didn't trust the bastard. Trent had nearly broken Emily's heart, and I just couldn't say that I could trust someone with little more than an apology as a gesture of reconciliation. He was her brother, she wanted to trust him, but that didn't mean I'd ever look at him without distrust in my heart.

"I'm going to lie down for a bit," Emily said when we walked into the penthouse. I knew her family time had worn her out, so I didn't protest. Right now, I thought I could use some alone time.

It had been astonishing how much noise could come from family gatherings. Even when my birth parents were alive, we'd never had gatherings like that. My mother was far too unstable even to consider it. She'd wrecked family dinners over the smallest things: a bug that flew by that told her we'd poisoned her food, or a speck of dust that she thought might be poison my father had put in mine.

Today had been … eye-opening. It wasn't just how many of them there was; it was the twins and their similarities, holding the baby, and talking to her parents. Who were very odd people, I'd decided, but got on with making conversation with them. They weren't necessarily cold, just a tad reserved. Kind of like my adoptive parents.

Emily's parents would warm to me, as the James couple had, and would lose some of that rigidness over time. I hoped. Her dad wasn't a man I wanted to make an enemy out of, no matter how old he was. I could feel it when he shook my hand. He might be elderly now, but he still had power.

The women, the subtle ways they guided their men was amusing, until I realized Emily did the same with me. I didn't mind, she'd made a huge difference in my life, she'd brought joy where there'd been sadness, but it was amusing to know she had womanly ways.

Then the babies.

I'd held a baby.

I could still feel his weight in my arms, soft but reassuring, while at the same time the most terrifying thing I'd ever done. That might have been the most amazing part of the day. Apart from how pleased Emily was on the drive home. She'd been quiet but smiling throughout the drive back to our place. That had been worth the headache that eventually developed between my eyes.

It would take some getting used to, being around her family, but I could do it. I'd have to, if I wanted to keep her in my life. Which was something else on its own.

I'd already made the decision that I wanted to keep her in my life, even if it might not be fair to her. I'd pushed her away for a long time, afraid of what it would mean, of what might change in my life. I hadn't realized that the changes would be good.

Yet, there was still the question of my health.

I poured a small glass of scotch, my medicine didn't allow any more than that, and watched as my hand shook when I picked the small glass up. The tremor didn't stop, as it usually did, and I felt a twinge in my back. I winced, put the glass down on the table, and sat on the couch.

My hand kept shaking as if something had taken control of my limb, and I tried to make it stop. I clenched my fist, shook my arm, stretched it over my head, but nothing made the tremor stop. Finally, just when I was about to get up and scream down the phone for my doctor, the tremor stopped.

I sighed, reached for the glass, and took a sip. The heat of the liquid burned down my throat, but I savored the sensation. I'd have to tell Emily. That's all there was to it. It was unfair not to tell her.

I decided I'd tell her the next day. I wanted one more night. Just in case, one more night snuggled up close to her. One night where she didn't look at me with pity or disgust. Just one more night of her loving touch.

I finished the drink and went into the bedroom. I dropped my clothes and slid into bed behind her, naked. She turned into my arms and wrapped herself in me.

"Decided to join me, did you?" she asked softly, sleepily.

"I couldn't stop thinking about you." I pushed my face into her neck and inhaled her scent.

"Mm, I'm glad. I was missing you too." Her hand moved down between us to grasp me in her hand. She was an expert now, and her touch was perfect.

I groaned when her hand tensed around me and began to move. Slow at first, easy to enjoy as the pleasure rippled through me. "Don't stop, Emily."

"As if I ever would," she whispered and moved away enough to trace kisses along my jaw.

I felt like a young boy, uncertain and unsure, as she moved along my body. Everything felt new all over again, and when her tongue circled around my nipple, I gasped. I'd forgotten how good that felt. She squeezed the small nipple, much smaller than her own, and licked the tip she held between her fingers.

A jolt shot through my dick, and I moaned.

The sensation mixed with the feelings that came

from her hand wrapped around my dick, and I wasn't certain I would last much longer. I held my hand over hers and pushed her back with my shoulder.

"Let me love you, Emily." I'd never said it to her before, not that I remembered, but it seemed right now. I wanted to worship her, to love her, even if I couldn't say the words to her.

I said I love you with the soft kiss I pecked on her lips. I told her how much I adored her when I sank my teeth into her neck and then licked. Her taste was nectar on my tongue, and so I moved down, to gather more of her unique tastes. She tasted like cherries along her neck, but her breasts tasted of the raspberries her tight nipples reminded me of.

I'd known a lot of women in my life, I'd fucked a lot of them, but none of them had ever been Emily. None of them had ever made me want to scream with something I had no way to define. I licked her nipple before I sucked it into my mouth. Her hips rushed up at me, hit my right hip, and I pushed her body down. My fingers dove into her folds, and I teased her there, my fingers a soft strum against her clit.

When she began to sigh my name and claw at my shoulders, I moved my hand so my palm would press into her clit, while my fingers delved inside of her. I stroked her, softly, then faster, following the pace of her breath at first.

When her breathing became erratic, when her skin was flushed and perspiration started to speckle along her skin, I sucked hard on her nipple. The effect was immediate, and her thighs clamped down on my hand. Her back arched, and I felt satisfaction throb in my dick. It was a beautiful sight to watch Emily come.

I thought women were afraid to let a man watch them really let go, but Emily had never been ashamed. She let go, her back arched, her head went back, and she forgot to breathe. It all made me even harder for her. That was what a woman's pleasure did to a real man. A boy might laugh, but a man drinks in the sight of his woman's pleasure. As I did now.

Emily's hands started to scratch at my shoulders, and I knew she wasn't done. I'd waited, I'd tried to hold myself back, but as she took off again, I lost my grip on my control.

I nudged her legs apart and sank into the heated depths of her. She was slick, hot, and so tight around me that I shuddered. It felt so good when I was inside Emily. She made me feel alive, like there was no end to life, and that we would live forever.

I pulled her legs around me and lifted her so that I could drive into her, straight to that spot that made her shoot off like a rocket. She writhed with me, her hips a blur, as she let her head fall back in total abandon.

Emily could be restrained, she could wait her turn,

but she didn't have to do any of that right now. She just had to take what I gave her.

She took it with both fists, greedily, as if she might never get it again.

I lost my stride for a minute but quickly retrieved it. Now wasn't the time for those thoughts, and I sank down into her again. Each thrust was warm, liquid pleasure, and the sensation of her as I left her, a grip that didn't want to let go, was just as exciting.

"Emily, I can't wait anymore, baby. Fuck, come with me, please." I thrust into her, hard, deep, and heard a soft sound, a sound that she only made on the best occasions. Surprise, pleasure, and then she almost turned inside out.

I was right there with her, lost in the way my dick was exploding over and over again. I didn't know I had it in me, but I did. After a while, I slumped against her, done, but still lost in bliss.

I rolled, pulled her on top of me, and held her as we tried to remember how to breathe. She was always the first one to recover, and she left the bed to get a glass of water. She brought me one and set it on my nightstand. She crawled in beside me and pulled the covers up.

"Maybe we should take a shower?" I said, too tired to actually do it.

"Tomorrow. I'm too fucking tired." She didn't swear

a lot, but it was cute when she did. It was also a sign of how tired she was.

"Good idea. Tomorrow." I patted her, but the word tomorrow was no real comfort.

Tomorrow I'd tell her that I might die and leave her alone. Tomorrow I'd tell her that it might be a long, slow process, and she'd have to watch me wither away to nothing. I might go blind; I might lose the ability to speak. I'd read about what could happen. I knew what my fate could be.

It wasn't pretty, it wasn't at all kind, what fate had in store for me. Not unless a new treatment came along. The medicines could control some of the symptoms, but there was no cure. Not yet.

I pulled her to me, the glass of water forgotten.

"Sleep well, Emily." I kissed her cheek, and she hummed.

"Sweet dreams, Dylan."

She might have been sweating ten minutes ago, but she was back to her normal, fruity smell. Pain arced through my gut as I wondered if she'd be in that spot tomorrow night. What if she walked out?

I couldn't imagine that. I was banking on her not running out on me, but she might. There was always a possibility of that. Not everyone was made to be a caretaker. Even if they were good with kids and managing people's lives. She'd actually taken care of her family her whole life. It wasn't fair to ask her to stick around and maybe face caring for me. Wasn't that where we were heading?

Wasn't the idea that we would be here for each other?

I didn't really have doubts about Emily, but I knew reality. I had to face reality. Life wasn't always fair, and sometimes people surprised you. I was sure the girl my father fell in love with shocked the fuck out of him when she suddenly turned into a psychotic harridan.

He'd expected a wife, a baby, and a quiet life. He hadn't got that at all. He'd got anything but peace. Mom had nearly driven us both mad with her own madness. Then, the ultimate shock, when she'd tried to kill us all. She'd only managed two of us. I'd escaped.

For the rest of my life, I'd avoided love, real commitment. What if I turned out to be like Mom? There'd been no signs of it, but she'd snapped one day. She hadn't been insane when Dad fell in love with her.

Which made me realize that Emily was a lot like my Dad. She was a giver, a caretaker, someone who gave everything she had to those she loved. It was a reassuring thought because deep down, I was really afraid to tell her what was wrong with me.

It was stupid, I knew that, but fuck, how did you ruin someone's day with the shit I had to drop on her? I rolled away and pressed my face into the side of my head where it had started to ache. I stared into the darkness of the room, lost in my own thoughts.

Then Emily rolled over to wrap around me. She sought me out even when she was asleep. I was positive she felt the same way about me, and calm finally settled over me. I was certain, at last, that she would support me. She wouldn't run away.

Emily wasn't the kind to do that, not unless she was pushed away. Although, I thought with a final happy thought, she'd pushed right back at me when I'd tried to push her away. She'd steamrolled into my life and squashed every protest I'd made. That wasn't a woman who would give up at the first sign of trouble.

I fell asleep then, at peace at last. I had a plan in place now. I knew what I needed to do. I almost felt relief. It would be over soon, the hiding I'd done, the dishonesty, a lot of people would call it. Tomorrow Emily would decide what our future would be. I was happy with that.

11

EMILY

"*Emily*, this is incredible," Jessi whispered to me as I ushered her into our penthouse. Her eyes were round with wonder, as if she'd never set foot into such a place before. I knew she had; she was my eldest brother's wife, after all.

"I just wanted it to feel less like a showroom and more like a home," I explained. The place was tastefully decorated, and I'd added little touches here and there. My wicker baskets along the baseboards in corners, a few prints I'd found on the walls, fluffy pillows and blankets on the couches; it all made it home to me.

"I knew you'd have a place like this," she whispered again, as Ember and Laura came in from the hot tub area in the back. "A place that feels like a home. Your parents' house is so ... untouchable."

"You're right, and the rooms at the resort that I

stayed in were nice, but they weren't home. This is home." I held my arms out for a moment and let them fall.

"Where's Dylan?" she asked as we moved into the kitchen. She inspected the vegetable tray I'd prepared and popped a cherry tomato in her mouth.

"Downstairs, busy at work, I suppose." He'd left early this morning, probably because he knew the ladies planned to come and visit me, and he wanted to give me some privacy.

"I guess he's like Trent and works all the time." She settled onto a bar stool, and my other sisters-in-law joined her.

"I guess all of our men do," I said with a soft laugh and filled glasses with sparkling water with the light hint of peach to give it some flavor.

"They do. Kevin's off to Tennessee again, can you believe it?" Ember said, and I glanced over at her. The sunlight had bleached her dark blonde hair to a lighter shade, and her eyes were shining with happiness. She was happy, despite the fact that Kevin was away.

"How's the album doing?" I asked her and leaned against the kitchen island between us. I knew I stood on that side to keep my distance from them, on some deeper level, but wasn't prepared to really think about it yet.

After all, it wasn't Ember's fault her new album had

exposed me. She hadn't contacted me either, and we used to talk at least once a week. I nibbled at the inside of my cheek as she told me about album sales and her tour dates. I only half-heard because I was too busy taking in how dang happy she looked.

I wanted that happiness, I hated to admit it, but the presence of these three women made me a little sad. They'd all done as their husbands had told them to do. They'd turned their backs on me. Anger, hurt, and tension rose the more I thought about it, until I was on the verge of telling them all to get out.

"Where's your bathroom, Em? I really need to go." Jessi came over to my side of the island and whispered, her delicate baker's hand on my elbow.

"This way," I said to her and headed out of the room. She knew me so well, and she'd seen that I needed a moment to catch my breath.

I took her to the bathroom, and we sat down on the edge of the tub together.

"Feel better?" she asked and took my hand.

"This is hard, Jessi. Harder than I thought it would be." I did the whispering this time, but it was mainly because my throat was so tight, I could barely speak. A tear slid out of my eye, and I wanted to disappear into the floor.

"I can't tell you how sorry I am, Emily. I should have told Trent to get over his fucking temper tantrum and I did, when I found out exactly why he was so upset with you that he … ahem"—she paused to clear her throat again before she went on—"that he basically threw the biggest hissy fit in the world and had your father disown you."

"I can't believe you used the word hissy fit and Trent together." I wiped at a tear and laughed.

"It's the truth. You were my friend when I was little, and your entire family told you no. You never gave up on me or turned your back on me. I did, even if I didn't realize I had for a while. I'm very sorry for that, Emily. I don't know if you can forgive me, obviously you're trying, and I hope you can. I love you, sister, and I always have." She put her arm around me then and we sat together for a moment in quiet.

"Come on, let's get out there before Laura and Ember eat all of those vegetables." We stood together, and I pulled her back for one last hug.

"Thank you, Jessi. I really needed that."

"Don't mention it. Listen, Laura and Ember, they aren't as forward as I am, so don't be upset with them if you don't get a similar apology from them, okay? Laura is so sweet, as you know, and she can be rather timid, as can Ember. Just know that they love you, but not as much as I do, because I've loved you a lot longer than they have." She grinned as she pulled back, wiped another stray tear away, and kissed my cheek.

"You do have a way of making things better, Jessi. You always did." I opened the bathroom door and we went out into the kitchen again.

"Hey, we wanted to apologize to you, Emily," Laura and Ember said at the same time as I came back in.

I glanced at Jessi with a secret smile. They had plucked up the courage to apologize after all. I smiled at them both, gave each one a hug, and went to sit on the other side of the island. Now, instead of a barrier, it was a way to keep the spotlight on me. I felt I could be more open with them now.

The elephant in the room had been mentioned and put to rest. We could get on with being friends again now.

"So what's Dylan like when he's at home?" Ember asked, her sultry voice always a delight to listen to. Whether she sang or simply spoke, her voice was music. She dipped a cucumber in the dip that I'd made and grinned a broad grin.

"He's the most amazing man, but then, I expect we all say that about the man of our dreams, don't we?" I sipped at my sparkling water and thought about how to answer them. "He's so domineering outside of these walls, especially when it comes to business. He's determined to be at the top. Driven even, but here at home? He's still driven to be his best, but he's kind, gentle, and always knows what I need."

"Aw," I heard from Laura and glanced at her. She was a fighter, far more than you could tell by looking at her.

She'd had breast cancer and survived it, and that made her a trooper in my book. Her skin was a little pale sometimes, but her classic beauty shone through her blue eyes and blonde hair. She was sweet, gentle, and kind, but she could also stand her ground when she needed to. She kept Mason on his toes and had changed him for the better. Until Trent threw his temper tantrum, that was.

"You deserve to be happy, Emily. It looks good on you," Jessi said, and I felt pride for some odd reason. I wasn't sure why, maybe because I'd fought so hard for that happiness, but I was proud of myself.

"Dylan the only thing that puts that glint in your eye?" Ember asked, always curious.

"I guess. I have a friend named Roxie; she's uh, well, a little different from us." Then I thought about the humble beginnings each of these ladies came from and amended my statement. "She's actually a lot like us. Tough, caring, but deserves a break."

"Oh, she sounds interesting." Laura leaned her elbows on the island and gave me her undivided attention.

"She's not had the finer things in life, not until now. She works hard for what she has, and she's accomplished everything on her own."

"What does she do?" Jessi prompted me to go on when I paused. I didn't want to tell Roxie's business, or Dylan's for that matter, but Roxie meant a lot to me, and I wanted to know these ladies would accept her. I wasn't ashamed of her, either, so I put it bluntly.

"She's an award-winning exotic dancer. She's known around the world for her talent." I'd seen the awards she'd won and knew the places she'd been to; I wasn't making up information about her or building her up more than she deserved.

"Really?" They all blurted and leaned even closer. I was fairly certain Jessi's feet weren't even on the bar stool anymore. "Have you seen her dance? That stuff looks amazing."

"I can show you videos of her," I offered and when they all nodded I picked up my tablet. I found the website her videos were on and selected one of the better-quality videos. All three of my sisters-in-law watched with amazement as Roxie did her stuff on a stage in the UK.

They were stunned, and I couldn't blame them; Roxie really was amazing. She was like a flower one minute, that blossomed into a feather, and then a sensually slithering snake as she climbed her pole, slid along it, and then fell before she broke her fall with nothing more than the pressure of her thighs.

"I can't believe it's possible to do that." Ember

watched, fascinated, and I knew they'd get along with Roxie just fine if she chose to meet them; she might not, and that was her prerogative. I wouldn't force it, but I wanted them to know about her.

"Does she perform out here?" Jessi broke my reverie, and I turned to face her as the video ended.

"Yeah, at a place called Elmo's; you probably haven't noticed it." All three women shook their heads in the negative, and I knew I'd have to ask Roxie if I could bring them out one night. They all wanted to see her perform. "I'll call her and ask if we can visit one night, just us four."

I didn't want to go to a club like Elmo's with my brothers in tow. That was just way too much ick for me. My sisters-in-law were fine, but my brothers? Nope, that wouldn't happen. I wouldn't even take Dylan when we went.

A sudden wave of nausea swamped me, and I leaned over to hold onto the island. I blinked until the nausea passed and looked up to see if any of them had noticed. Of course, they all had.

"Sorry, I've been having migraines and the medicine sometimes makes me sick." I didn't want to tell them yet, but I could see each one speculating, looking for a clue. I wouldn't be able to hide the pregnancy from Dylan for long with these three around, so I knew I'd have to tell him soon.

"Well, don't work too hard if you're getting migraines, Emily." Jessi stood up to fill her glass with more of the sparkling water and patted my back. "Not in your condition."

"Jessi!" I spluttered at her whisper, but she had a totally blank face, as if she hadn't said anything at all. I glared at her for a minute but grinned. "I'll be careful."

"Well, I think we should do this again, but I have to get going. I have a plane to catch," Ember said and stood up.

"Oh, not so soon!" I protested, but I knew she had commitments.

"It can't be helped, but I'm glad to see you again, Emily. You look fantastic." She kissed each side of my face, and I walked with her to the door. "I am sorry, you know."

"Don't worry about it, Ember. All is forgiven." I meant it. The past was finished when it came to these three. My brothers might have to do a bit more groveling, though.

As well as my parents. Those two really needed a kick in the pants, but I doubted it would change them at all. They were who they were, and that was how they'd stay. Unbending, unyielding, and forever conservative. They'd die of embarrassment if they knew the things I'd done. I wouldn't change any of my actions since I'd found out I could have a life too.

Laura and Jessi left about an hour later. It had all done me a lot of good, and I texted Roxie to let her know how it had all gone. She replied that she was glad, and she wanted to come and see me. I agreed and met her downstairs for lunch in my office. The vegetables and dip hadn't filled me up.

I cleared the table in my office, and a waiter brought in a tablecloth and the food we'd ordered. It was delicious, as I knew it would be, and we talked about the day we'd had so far. She hadn't been up long, but she'd managed to get some work done for the charity we both volunteered for, and she'd been there most of the morning.

"It's odd to see you in jeans and a t-shirt with no makeup on," I mentioned with a smile. "You look good like that."

"Ah, my glamour is gone when I'm like this. I look like a normal woman." She brushed off my compliment, but I wasn't about to have it.

"Roxie, you're beautiful, and without the makeup your skin shines through. You look wonderful, healthy, and alive. So many women look washed out without makeup on, but it suits you." Her normally black-rimmed blue eyes stood out even more without the eyeliner, and she looked more approachable.

I guess for her the makeup was a mask to hide behind, but also a shield against the world. She hadn't had an easy life, but she'd made something of herself, despite all of that.

"Nathan likes it too," she said softly and peeked up at me from beneath her lashes.

"Who is Nathan?" I gushed and leaned in toward her.

"He's a man I met at the charity. He's really … nice." Her smile was tentative but happy.

I stared at her, stunned. "He's not from the club?"

"No, but he knows what I do. He's fine with it." She brushed her hair out of her eyes and looked away. "He's great, Emily. I think you'll like him."

"If he makes you smile like that, Roxie, I know I will." I took her hand, happy for the woman who needed to be loved so much more than she ever let on. I hoped she'd finally found it.

12

EMILY

"Roxie has a boyfriend," I said that night as Dylan and I changed the bed linen. "She's really happy."

I'd had the other woman on my mind since she'd left earlier in the day. I really was happy for her and wanted her to experience what I'd found with Dylan. Alright, our beginning hadn't exactly been perfect, we'd struggled against each other, but we'd finally come to terms with who we were and what we needed to do.

That hadn't been easy, but we'd managed it. We still had an issue or two to work through, I thought as I felt a pang of hunger growl in my stomach, but I thought we could handle it all. Together, we could handle most things.

Dylan had shown me that as he accepted my family into his life. He didn't have to do that; he could have just dismissed them, refused to meet with them, and refused to allow my sisters-in-law to come here. He'd known I needed my family and had not only accepted it, but made an effort to be part of that group of people.

It mattered to me, I thought as I smoothed a flat sheet over the fitted sheet and then reached for the pillows.

"Oh? That's great. Is he a boyfriend-boyfriend or an Elmo's-boyfriend?" I knew he wasn't judging Roxie, just curious. He looked up at me, his eyes curious and I thought, not for the first time, how handsome he was.

It made my heart squeeze sometimes, when I looked at him. It was love, I knew that, but still, we hadn't said those words. One day, we would. Maybe not tonight. I remembered he'd asked me about Roxie's new boyfriend after a moment and made a goofy face at myself.

"Sorry, you distracted me with that handsome face of yours. He's a real boyfriend. You should see how she looks when she talks about him." I sighed and pulled a pillow into a pillowcase. "She looks like a fairy princess or something."

"You always look like that, Emily. Or like a little nymph." He came over to my side and grabbed me to tickle me. With a laugh of joy, we fell to the bed. Only Dylan wasn't laughing when we hit the mattress.

In fact, he was very, very quiet. I turned around and

pushed him back, afraid that I'd somehow hurt him. "Dylan? What's wrong?"

"Emily, my..." He looked terrified, and his hand gripped at his leg frantically. His eyes caught mine, and I could see stark fear in their depths. "I can't feel my legs."

"What?" I was too stunned to take it in or panic too much. He couldn't feel his legs? Why not? What had I done? "What have you done?"

"It's, fuck, call an ambulance, darling. Hurry, please." He fell back against the bed, his face scrunched with some emotion, fear, pain, I didn't know, I just knew he'd asked for an ambulance, and he wouldn't joke about that.

I picked up my phone but urgency suddenly made my fingers misdial 911 two times before I got it right. I held my breath until a voice answered in a calm voice.

"911, what's your emergency?"

"My boyfriend, we were making the bed, and well, he just fell over. He can't feel his legs now."

"Okay, ma'am, do you want me to send an ambulance?" I could hear the sound of keys being tapped on the other end of the line.

"Yes, please."

I gave the woman at the call center our address and explained that I didn't know what to do now.

"What's your name, ma'am?" she asked softly, and I took a deep breath that calmed me a little.

"My name is Emily. His is Dylan. Is there something I should be doing? Put ice on it?"

"No, Emily, just wait for the paramedics. Don't try to force him to move or anything. Just keep him calm for me, alright?"

"Of course," I answered but felt useless as I reached over to touch Dylan again, just to reassure myself he was alright.

Dylan was having a hard time breathing, and I was afraid that whatever was wrong would make him stop breathing altogether. "Dylan, what's wrong?"

"I can't really explain," he gritted out between clenched teeth. "Here, while we're waiting for them to get here, call this doctor for me. Tell him my name and that I need him out here, tonight. Cost is of no importance. Just tell him to get here."

He handed me his phone from the pocket of his t-shirt, and I did as he told me, while he kept the 911 dispatcher informed about his condition. A man answered the phone, and I explained who I was and what Dylan had said. The doctor promised he'd be on the next flight out and hung up. I stared over at Dylan, afraid, confused, but most of all, stunned at how the playful moment had changed into this.

"Did you hit your head? Is that what's wrong?" I moved over him, but he pushed me down gently.

"No, Emily. I, well, you'll find out soon enough." He

leaned back on the bed, and I could see how nervous he was, how afraid.

"Are you in pain?" I asked, afraid to move in case it increased his pain.

"Not really, no. It's more numbness than pain. Although, oddly, that does kind of hurt, the numbness. You'd think it wouldn't." He stared at the ceiling, and I felt my heart break. What was wrong with him?

I didn't have a lot of time to worry because I heard the elevator come up to the penthouse and went out to let the paramedics in. They came in with a stretcher, greeted me politely, and asked where Dylan was. It was only then that I realized how bad it was. He couldn't even sit up on the bed. I wondered then if he'd actually pulled me down to the bed earlier or if he'd simply fallen with me in his arms.

One of the paramedics, a dark-haired man around Dylan's age, with kind eyes and blue gloves on his hands, asked him a series of questions. That's when I heard Dylan finally admit what was wrong.

"I was diagnosed with MS earlier this year. I volunteered for a new drug trial, and well, I can't get up now, as you can see." He tried to joke about it, but I could see real fear in his eyes.

I couldn't blame him. I'd be screaming to be taken to the hospital right away if it was me. The two men soon had Dylan on a stretcher, and I put on a pair of jeans and threw a jacket over my cotton nightgown before I grabbed my purse. I followed them down, then took my car to meet them at the hospital.

The drive to the hospital was nerve-wracking, but I followed behind the ambulance and that ensured traffic wasn't a problem. It wasn't long before the ambulance pulled into the emergency room, and I drove into the parking lot to find a place to park. I locked the doors on the car and hurried into the emergency waiting area. All I could do was sit and wait, I was told. So that's what I did.

I wasn't allowed in the waiting area they put Dylan in, but later, when he'd been admitted and put into a room a nurse came to get me.

"He's asking for you, ma'am," the nurse said, a kind smile in place. It must have been something healthcare professionals practiced. I was glad for it, either way, because I was shaken badly and scared out of my mind.

I walked into Dylan's private room to find him connected to machines by cables and tubes. He had his eyes closed, and the bed was in an upright position. That couldn't be comfortable. I moved to stand beside the bed to try to figure out how to move it down so he'd be comfortable.

"Emily?" he asked, his voice scratchy. I looked around and saw a plastic pitcher with water in it on a tray by his bedside. I poured some in the plastic cup on the tray and gave it to him.

"I'm here, darling," I assured him and sat down.

"Fuck. I was going to tell you, I swear." He opened his eyes, and I could see how worried he was. "Please don't leave me."

"Dylan? Why the hell would I leave you? You're ill, not married with five children. Now that, I'd leave you for, but this? Baby, no. You need me, and I'll be here for you. I swear that to you." I put the rail on his bed down and sat next to him. I put my hand over his heart and looked at him. "I'm not a monster, you know?"

He let his head fall back on the pillow and sighed. "I was worried enough about my past, that you might think I was like my mom, but this too? Fuck, Emily, you're an angel. I always knew you were, but you just proved it."

I kissed his cheek but held my weight off of him. "What have they said?"

"That I'm having a flare. They're giving me medicine that should take care of the problem, but there's never a guarantee with this disease. I may end up worse, before it gets better. Or I might ... well, this could kill me, Emily."

"I know, Dylan. I read about it while I waited to see you. I'll be here for you, through whatever comes, and

I'll make sure you have the best care you need, if I bank-rupt myself and my family to do it."

"I don't think it'll go that far." He laughed softly and looked up at me. "I have good insurance and a little money of my own."

"You do. I'm just so used to…" I let the words trail off, slightly embarrassed. I'd been privileged my whole life but knew others hadn't.

"It's alright, baby. I know what you meant."

He sighed and closed his eyes again. "Why don't you go home, Emily? Get some rest? I'll probably be in here for a few days, and you need to rest."

"I do, but I'll stay here with you. I'm not leaving your side." I looked at the uninviting chair meant to also serve as a bed for family members. It would have to do.

Throughout the night, nurses came and went, and Dylan was wheeled out twice for different tests that couldn't wait until morning. During one of the tests, Dylan's doctor came into the hospital room, the doctor he had flown in from Kansas.

"Hi, I'm Emily, his girlfriend," I said when the doctor introduced himself.

We talked about what would happen with Dylan, what other tests they'd run, and whether the doctor was hopeful Dylan would be home by tomorrow.

"I doubt it. I suspect he's having what we call an

attack or a flare. I want to keep an eye on him, and the best place to do that is here."

"Alright," I agreed and looked away. I was embarrassed to admit I'd forgotten the doctor's name already. It was three in the morning, though.

"You should go home, Emily. There isn't a lot you can do here," the doctor said, and I nodded.

"Probably, but I can't. I won't leave him on his own." I'd listened to the man down that hall and the way he screamed, and I knew it was better to stay with Dylan. The sounds and noises in a hospital were stressful enough when you had someone with you; alone the stress was just amplified.

"Fine, but try to rest when you can. We don't need two patients." The doctor patted my arm and told me he was off to find the admitting doctor to speak to. I settled back into the chair and pulled the thin blanket a nurse had brought me up around my neck.

I still had my nightgown on, I realized, but I didn't care. Dylan needed me. I wasn't as afraid as I'd been when I first arrived at the hospital, but I was fully aware that Dylan needed help that I couldn't give him. From what I'd read, I knew he would experience stages with the disease, if his medicine didn't control the way the disease wreaked havoc on Dylan's brain and nerves.

I'd be doing a lot more research as the days came and went. I'd know this disease backward and forward before long, but for now, I knew enough to be afraid, but not terrified. There was hope he could have a normal life.

I patted my stomach, totally aware now that Dylan might not want to have children. He might be afraid to. That added to my worry. He'd looked so wonderful with that baby in his arms, that I'd started to think that he would be happy about my news. Now, I had to wonder. Would it be fair to dump this on him at such a bad time in his life?

Or would it give him a reason to fight?

The orderlies wheeled Dylan back into the room and helped him get into the position he desired on the bed. He was a very fit and healthy man so he could maneuver his upper body well, he just had no control over his legs. My heart broke as this strong man struggled.

Normally, he'd be too prideful to let me see him at this moment in his life. He wouldn't want me to see how weak he was. This was a different Dylan than the one I'd met, though. This Dylan needed help and didn't mind taking it. He had no choice, so he accepted it without complaint.

"How are you, darling?" I asked from the side of the bed. I stood close enough to brush his hair back from his face and watched him as he struggled to open his eyes.

"I'm so tired, Emily. So fucking tired. I'm glad you're here." He clasped the hand that brushed at his hair and kissed it. "Come up here. Sleep with me. I need to feel you."

I wanted to protest but didn't. He wanted to feel me next to him. I went to the side with the least amount of cables and no tubes and curled up against him. He sighed and fell asleep immediately.

I wasn't awake for very long after that. It had been a long, exhausting day, followed by a much longer night. I still hadn't taken it all in, but I was happy because I was able to feel him beside me as the night faded away.

13

EMILY

When life hands you lemons, you're supposed to make lemonade. That was how the saying went, and it was all I could do now. Make the best of a bad situation. The problem wasn't that Dylan was ill, it was that I felt helpless. His condition grew worse throughout the day, and his vision became blurry.

Doctors, nurses, consultants and specialists came and went into his room, each one serving a different purpose. One came to check his eyes after he was given more medicine; another came to check how his bladder was holding up. Then another specialist came in to consult with the doctor who had already assessed Dylan's eyes. It was all very confusing, and I forgot names at the drop of a hat.

It wasn't that I didn't care about their names; it was

that I couldn't keep up. I was exhausted, and the pregnancy only added to that. I got sick after I had breakfast, and thankfully Dylan was out for another test when that happened. A nurse came in, a brown-haired woman with warm brown eyes, and she asked me if I was alright. I said I was as I wiped my face with those awful paper towels then threw them away.

"If you need anything, just let me know, sweetie. I know what it's like. I have three of my own."

I stared at the woman, surprised that she knew.

"You have that look; it's unmistakable, if you know it. You have to take care of yourself now, and this is going to be trying for both of you. I'm here if you need anything."

I felt a wavering smile stretch across my lips and nodded. She left before I could say a word, but I felt that sense of understanding that women shared sometimes. That knowing that came with things like pregnancy, marriage, and most things woman. It made me feel warm.

I sat in that horrible chair that was quickly becoming my nightmare and waited for Dylan's return. I flicked on the television and found a load of early morning cartoons. I saw one that was far older than me, but I enjoyed it because it was a classic. I wasn't really paying it much attention, but it was distracting, at least.

When Dylan came in, I helped him to settle in his

bed, washed his face and arms with a sponge the nurse brought me, and checked him over visually. I saw warm skin, strong limbs, and eyes that were bleary, but alert.

"How are your eyes, darling?" I asked him, and he gave me a wan smile.

"Still blurry. Not quite double vision, but enough to make my stomach feel sick." He closed his eyes, and I knew it was to seek relief from the nausea his condition caused. "I need to get back to work; I don't have time for this."

"You do have time, that's why you've hired so much staff. I'll make a few phone calls in a bit and make sure everything's in order. Don't worry, Dylan, we'll get you through this." I squeezed his hand and sat on the edge of his bed. "You don't have to do everything alone, you know."

"I do know," he said and opened his eyes for a moment to smile at me. He closed them, though, and turned his head away. "As soon as I can think, I'll give you a list of people to call. I just need my head to stop spinning."

His Kansas doctor, a very good man, and good at his job, had him on yet another new medicine. One that was supposed to be the next best thing to a miracle for those who suffered from MS. I had hope but tried to be realistic.

"Take your time, darling. I'm going to go out and

make a few phone calls, then I'll be back. Get some rest." I kissed the side of his head and left the room. He was asleep before I made it out of the door.

I ran straight into my brothers, Trent, Mason, and Kevin.

"What are you doing here?" I asked, as I led them away from his door.

"I heard what happened and came to find out if you needed anything. We came to find out, that is," Trent amended when Mason and Kevin looked at him with twin glares.

"I know a couple of people who work here, Emily, and they told me that you were here with a friend. I knew it must be Dylan, and I hope you don't mind. We were just trying to be supportive." Mason came to me and gave me a hug.

"Of course, you know some of the staff here," I mumbled as I buried my head in his shoulder, tears suddenly in my eyes. His wife had been a patient at one point in time, as she fought her battle with cancer. It would make sense that he might know some of the staff here. "I'm so glad you are all here."

"Don't cry, little sister. We'll make this better. Somehow." Kevin patted my back, and I turned to hug him.

"Thank you just being here is wonderful of you all." I moved on to Trent. He was always so awkward when he first hugged you, but then, he would settle into it and gave off such comforting vibes. They all did, really.

"Just tell us what to do, Emily. How can we help?" Trent pulled away, tilted my face up, and gave me a brotherly kiss on the forehead.

Now that was new. I blinked at him and smiled with a watery smile. "This, this is awesome. Really."

I let my head fall to his shoulder and hugged him tight. I'd thought I'd never have a hug from him again, but at last, he'd thawed.

"Tell me what's going on. Us, tell us." Trent had been given yet another glare by my other brothers, and I laughed at them all.

"Come to the family waiting area, and I'll explain it all."

Kevin stopped at the coffee stand in the large waiting area and brought us all a cup of standard, awful, hospital coffee. We all drank it anyway, as I began to explain what was wrong.

"So this could happen again?" Trent asked after I'd given him the rundown of Dylan's condition.

"It could, as he progresses through the stages of MS. He's teetering on the edge of second stage now, but his doctors are trying to prevent him from going over. Right now, he'll have tremors, problems with memory, maybe even urinary dysfunction, muscle pain and weakness. That might be all he ever experiences. There's no cure, that we know."

"I'll get one of my assistants researching around the globe, Emily; don't you worry," Trent interrupted, but then went quiet, his eyes intent on mine.

"Thank you. Thank you for being here, really. All of you."

Mason, always the joker, was quiet now. I knew he was thinking of Laura, and I took his hand. "You of all people will know what this is like. Thank you for being so brave."

"What? It's not brave at all." He brushed off the compliment but squeezed my hand. It was brave, to face coming into a place like the one where Laura had fought for her life and might have to fight for it again one day.

"Why don't you go home and get some rest, Emily? We'll stay here with Dylan until you come back."

"What?" I asked and turned to Kevin. "Don't you all have things to do, stuff to take care of?"

"That's what we have employees for, sis. We're here for you, as long as you need us." Kevin patted my hair and kissed my cheek.

I stared at them all, and for the first time in my life, I felt like my brothers really loved me. Tears burst from my eyes, and I sobbed an ugly sound that was actually happy. Kind of.

"Oh, Emily, honey, we're so sorry we've been such

horrible brothers to you." Trent moved to the couch I was on with Kevin and took me in his arms.

It might not be the most perfect time for a family reunion, but it was the right time. I had been so busy pretending that everything would be fine, that I'd almost convinced myself that I believed it. With them there, reality hit, and I took the comfort they offered me.

"Don't you worry, Emily, we'll make sure he recovers, one way or another," Mason volunteered when my sobs had tapered off, and I could focus again.

Trent handed me a handkerchief, and I mopped my face dry and sniffled until I'd recovered myself.

"Trust you to still use handkerchiefs," I joked as I reached for a box of tissues at the table beside me. I cleared up any remaining tears and threw the tissues away.

"Go home. Have a shower and rest. I know it won't be easy, but you have to stay strong. We'll get you both through this."

"Alright. I don't want to, but I know you're right."

"I'll call my driver. He's waiting for you," Trent said and moved away to make the call.

"We'll tell him where you are. We'll take care of him, I swear." Kevin hugged me tight, and that's when I noticed something.

None of them were in their normal suits. All had on jeans, loafers, and t-shirts. They'd come casual, prepared to be here for a while. They'd done this together then, I decided, and felt another wave of tears start, but swallowed it back.

I went back to the penthouse and did as instructed. I had a shower, a light lunch, and then went to bed. I didn't sleep, not at first; my brain was too exhausted, too nervous to sleep. I put on a movie, an old black and white film, and tried to watch it, but found my eyes kept closing.

I woke up a few hours later and realized I'd missed the movie. A color film was on, and the sky had started to darken. I rolled onto my back and stared up at the ceiling. I had to get dressed and head back to the hospital, but first, I had to wait for the nausea to pass.

I rubbed my hand over my still flat stomach and talked to the baby hiding inside of me. "You have to stop making me sick, little one. You're no bigger than a jelly bean, you know? Settle down in there."

The sickness passed after a few minutes, and I got up. I checked my phone and saw I had messages. My brothers told me that Dylan had improved and that he was going to be released later that night. His vision was better, his legs were working again, and he was responding well to the medicine. I wanted to cheer to the rooftops but held myself in check.

Dylan might not be out of the woods, but he'd improved enough that the doctors agreed that he could go home to recuperate. That was a good thing and one I'd be thankful for.

I also had a message from Roxie, and I sent a long one back to explain what had happened. She replied immediately and asked what I needed. She'd always been such a good friend. I replied saying all I needed was some love, and she sent that back gladly in her next text. I smiled as I got dressed and couldn't help but take stock.

I had my brothers and their wives in my life again, and Roxie, a true friend through it all. I had Dylan. I'd felt so alone not that long ago, and now, I almost had more love than I knew what to do with.

In fact, my sisters-in-law showed up just as I started to leave. "What are you all doing here?"

"Trent said you all were bringing Dylan home later, so we want to make sure you have what you need when you get back. Do you want us to pick up shopping, or make something to eat? What do you need, Emily? Just say the word." Jessi hugged me and went to the kitchen, Laura and Ember on her trail.

"Well, I could use some shopping, yes. I can order it; you don't have to go to that trouble, honey." I followed the women into my kitchen and tried to hold back tears again. "Dammit, Jessi, Laura, and Ember. Don't make me cry again. I've done enough of that today. I'll get one of those nasty headaches crying always gives me."

"Nope, no tears, sweetheart," Laura said, brusque as usual, but always loving. "Tell us what you need."

I sat at the table with them, and we decided on the things we might need here once Dylan was home. Ember went off to find the mattress made from some kind of special gel that one of the doctors had recommended. Jessi went to get groceries and planned to come back to make a dinner for all of us, and Laura decided to pick up the medicines the doctors had prescribed him. They would all meet back here and take care of everything.

I kissed each woman, each sister, and then I left. Trent's driver was waiting for me when I got downstairs and soon had me back at the hospital. I walked in to find the men talking quietly, but happily.

"Ah, there's Emily." Kevin stood up to let me get by him so I could kiss Dylan hello.

"How are you, darling?" I asked as I brushed hair back from his forehead.

"Tired, ready to go home. We were waiting on you. Everything's done, and I'm ready to go." He smiled at me, tired but happy.

"Shouldn't they keep you for one more night?" I asked, but he put his hand over my mouth and smiled.

"Don't give them ideas! There's no immediate danger of death. I'm improving, and I'm taking up space someone else might need. It'll be fine, Emily. Don't worry."

I stared back at him, my eyes narrowed. "Did you demand to go home, is that it?"

"No!" he protested but kept his smile. "There's really no point in my being here now, honey. I promise. It's going to be alright. I'll need some help to get out of bed, and time to heal, but I'll be fine."

"If you say so." I still wasn't sure, now that I was back in the hospital.

I'd wanted him to come home, but this seemed like too quick of a discharge. He could move again, and he proved that by sliding out of the bed. He was already dressed, he even had his shoes on, but it just seemed to be too soon.

I looked at my brothers, and they all nodded. "Fine, but I don't like it."

"It'll be fine, Emily. I promise." Dylan pulled me to him, and I let myself lean into him.

"It better be. Or you're coming right back here, mister.

14

EMILY

I stared at the black and white image on the screen, my heart full of love and wonder. "That's my baby?"

"It is. I'd say your approximately six weeks, Emily," the doctor said and gave me a grin. "Do you want pictures?"

"Yes, please." I sighed the words out, too caught up in watching the tiny creature inside of me to speak any louder. "It's amazing."

"Soon we'll be able to do a scan where you can see the face and body. It won't be 100 percent perfect, but you'll get an idea of what your baby looks like."

I nodded, still engrossed in my baby. My ears were attuned to the sound of its little heartbeat, faster than my own but steady. The doctor reassured me it was normal for the baby's heart to beat so fast, when it frightened me.

"Right, you'll need to set up another appointment to check how things are progressing. Watch what you eat. You stopped the Topamax, right?" She looked over at me, and I nodded quickly.

"Good, it has been known to cause some issues." She looked at me, took stock of my demeanor, and then carried on. "Cleft palette is an issue, one we need to watch for, since you were taking it during the first few weeks."

"Cleft palette? Oh no!"

"The options for children born with cleft palette have increased over the years and can do wonders. I wouldn't have told you, but you need to be aware, there is a possibility."

"I didn't know." I'd said this so many times lately that I was starting to feel like I was in a time loop. My baby might have a deformity.

I would love it no matter what, but the news hit me hard. Especially with Dylan's revelation. It had been two weeks since he came home, and he'd improved dramatically, but still. It had weighed on my mind, especially with the baby. How would he handle it if he stuck around?

I didn't see why he wouldn't; after all, I'd stuck by his side, even when I knew about his illness. Would he give me that same kind of love; I had to wonder? Deep down, I knew he would; I trusted him, after all. He was the one person I knew I could trust over the last few months. Why would he stop being the one I could go to now?

Sure, he was dealing with a lot of things right now—the new resort, his health, me, but he would have to know soon. There wasn't any denying that.

I dressed myself after the doctor left me and went out to my car. I got in and took the folder out of my purse, the one that had the first pictures of my baby inside. Our baby, I thought as I outlined the baby's form with my finger. Little more than a shape at the moment, but I could see where the body would form. It was real and growing, ready for life.

I started the car and drove to my favorite restaurant. I was meeting Jessi there. She was the only one who knew, although I had never quite confirmed anything to her. Like the nurse at the hospital, Jessi had intuited my pregnancy. I knew she'd ask me about it before long.

I wasn't wrong, I found out, when she walked into the restaurant and sat beside of me.

"Have you told him yet?" It was the first thing that came out of her mouth as she leaned over to kiss my cheek.

"No. I don't know how to. He has so much going on. I don't even know if he'll want it."

"I know how you feel. How do you think I felt when

I had to tell Trent I was pregnant?" I could tell from the way she sighed that she knew exactly how I felt. As if the world might come to an end once the news was out. "I can tell you, it's better to get it over with. If you don't, it will eat you up inside, and you'll start to resent him. Take your time, but you'll have to tell him soon."

I knew she spoke from experience. It wouldn't be easy, but I knew I had to tell him soon. Especially since the nausea had increased throughout the day. It wasn't just the mornings now; it could hit at any time. The cravings were insane.

"Is it normal to crave Ranch salad dressing?" I asked her quietly, as I looked over the menu.

"Women crave the strangest things when they're pregnant. I wouldn't touch bananas usually, but I ate a ton of them while I was pregnant." She picked up her menu and started to look it over.

"I don't want it on salad or food. I just want to drink bowls of it." The thought should be disgusting, but it actually made me hungry. This was all quite strange to me, and I hadn't had anyone to talk to about it. It was nice to have someone listen now.

"I wouldn't advise that; it can't be good for you." Jessi laughed. "Maybe just have some on salad, even if you don't want the salad."

"I guess. I know I have to eat healthy, but all I want is the salad dressing and tuna. I hate tuna. At least I liked the dressing before the pregnancy," I mumbled and tried to find something to eat from the menu.

"Have you found out when you're due yet?" she asked it casually, but I knew she was paying attention. Laura would be expecting her baby, and it would be nice to share the experience with her.

"I'm six weeks, so seven and a half months." It was a question I knew I'd have to get used to.

"After Laura then. That's good. Both of you at the same time would be a nightmare." She laughed and I joined her.

"The family would go mad. With all the babies, I doubt anyone will notice when it's my turn." It wasn't a complaint, but I did feel a little sad that there might not be much excitement about my baby.

"Are you kidding? That whole stunt you pulled with getting your own place really shook your brothers up. Especially after Trent pulled his hissy fit over it." She looked away, as if embarrassed, but then she grinned. "They're so much more helpful now and, well, you saw them at the hospital. I think you broke that final wall they all had."

"You think so?" I asked, eager to hear more about how my brothers had reacted to my demand for respect.

"I know so." She took a sip of water and looked at me. "They realize their little sister felt used, and to be fair, we sisters-in-law realized it too. It was wrong of us to expect so much from you. You were right to do what you did, Emily. So right."

The conversation drifted as the waiter brought our order.

"This Roxie friend of yours? When can I meet her?" Jessi's eyes glittered with interest, and I wondered how curious Jessi really was.

"Why?" I asked her, just to see her reaction.

"I watched some more of her videos. She's amazing. Maybe I'm curious about that place she works at."

"It's a very"—I paused and took a breath—"very interesting place. There's a lot more that happens there, but it's kept very quiet."

"I imagine it would have to be." She put her fork down, wiped her mouth, and sat back. "Places like that aren't very common, but Trent's taken me to a few. I just didn't know about that one."

"Really? Stuffy old Trent in a place like that? I don't want to picture it ... actually, never mind. Don't tell me more." I held a hand up to her, and we laughed together.

It felt good to laugh with her. It had been so long, but now, those months apart had melted away. We were the same friends we'd always been. I pushed my plate away, full at last, and looked over at her.

"Do you want to go shopping with me? I need to get a new dress, and while I have the sitter with the kids, I might as well get that done too."

"Sure, I don't have anything else planned this afternoon. Oh, Jessi? Do you want to see the pictures of the baby?" I had forgotten about the folder in my bag but took it out.

"Oh, look at that tiny little angel." Her voice held awe, and when she looked up, I saw tears in her eyes. "I'm so happy for you. You deserve to be happy and with a family of your own, Emily."

"Thank you." I squeezed her hand, and we got up to leave. The bill was paid, and we went out to her car. She drove us to a shop nearby, and I was drawn to their maternity section.

Jessi came with me as I looked at all the clothes that had been made for a woman's expanding belly. I felt stupidly happy. I'd need clothes like these soon enough, and she'd be there with me. That did my heart a lot of good.

"It's awful how much you cry when you're pregnant," I whispered and ducked my head.

"It's terrible, isn't it? You feel like you've constantly sprung a leak or something." She handed me some tissues out of her bag, and I wiped my face. "Do you want to get some of these?"

"Not yet. I think I should wait until I need them, don't you?" I didn't want to jinx anything and kept the rest of the sentence to myself. Now that I'd seen my baby growing in my stomach, I wanted to protect it more than ever.

"Might be a good idea. You've got time. Although, things will start to change other than your stomach size, you know?" She looked at me knowingly as we walked to the dress department. She began to list things off that could happen.

"I thought this process was all about glowing and blossoming? Not turning into a nightmare." I looked at her with dread, and she looked ashamed.

"Sorry, I didn't mean to scare you. I just thought you should know. I thought the same thing. Roses and flowers and all that bullshit. Not always."

"You're right, I guess, I should know what to expect."

"There's a book you can get, with a similar title to that. I'd recommend it. Takes some of the surprise out of things."

"I'll have a look for it." Maybe I'd get an electronic copy of it, I decided. A physical copy would be a dead giveaway, and I didn't want that to be the way Dylan found out.

I knew the time was coming, but the longer I waited, the harder it became. I wasn't exactly afraid of his response, but I didn't want to shock him into another episode, or make his head explode from stress. The poor man had a lot on his plate.

Jessi found the dress she wanted, and we left soon

after that. She took me back to my car, and I drove home. Dylan was downstairs, doing some paperwork. Not much had changed at home, and he had started to exercise again. We had a new gel-topped mattress, just in case he needed it, and I liked it, so we'd kept it on.

He'd had handles installed in the shower, and rails along the walls, just in case he slipped or lost his balance, but other than that, we tried to get back to normal. For now, he was improving every day, and I wanted to keep it that way.

I put down my bag and went into the kitchen.

I had started dinner and was at the island, scrolling through the book Jessi had recommended when I got a call from Roxie.

"Hey, you wanted to meet up tomorrow?"

"Yeah, if you want to. My sister-in-law wants to meet you. Only if you want to. I'm not going to force you into anything you don't want to do."

"Nah, it's fine, girl. I meet people every day, remember? I'll charm her pants off and satisfy her curiosity."

"I know you will." I smirked. Roxie was just talented like that. "Do you want to meet at the beach place or somewhere else?"

"No, that's fine. Good food, and I can run off if she starts to get weird on me."

"I'm sorry you have to worry about that." I sighed. "I

doubt Jessi will embarrass herself like that. She's pretty level-headed and not a judging kind of person."

"We'll see." She sounded doubtful, but not upset. "Lunchtime good for you?"

"That's fine. It's not too early for you?"

"No, not working tonight. I took a little time off to spend with Nathan."

"Oh dear. It is serious then."

"It's fucking freaking me out, if I'm honest. I can't say no to him. It's gross, Emily. Really gross."

"Love is not gross, Roxie!" I barked out with a laugh. "Come on, chill out. Enjoy it."

"I think I remember you saying similar words to me at one point, missy."

"I probably did. I take it all back. It's not gross at all. It's wonderful, awesome, and should be enjoyed fully."

"Dang, you're going to make me sick. Stop it!" I heard a mock gagging sound. "I'll see you tomorrow. Minus the attitude, please."

"You'll get twice as much for that," I promised her and hung up. It was nice to have someone to tease about love.

15

EMILY

I sat at the table and waited for my two best friends to show up. I had on a light blue summer dress, the temperature had soared early this morning, and a pair of sandals. I hadn't felt like putting on makeup but had on eyeliner and some lip gloss. My hair was piled up in a sloppy, but artful, mess on top of my head, and I wanted to just go to sleep and make it messier.

I'd promised to meet these two, however, so I waited patiently. The morning had been really long, but I knew my assistant, a newly hired fella named Neil, had taken one look at me and had started to field calls for me. That was his job anyway, but until this morning, I'd tried to handle everything that came my way. Today, I didn't protest. I let him turn callers away, and sat in my office, a cold glass of ginger ale and some crackers on my desk.

I wished there was a medicine to handle this part of pregnancy. I'd give anything to have it. I remembered there'd been something brought out at some point in time that had caused birth defects and felt guilt sting at my heart. I was already worried about my little jelly bean because of the medicine I'd taken for the migraines. I didn't want to add to it.

I'd read about cleft palate some more, after Dylan had gone to sleep last night. It worried me, it made me hurt that I might have caused the defect in my baby, but I was trying not to freak out too much. Roxie showed up just as the waiter brought me more ginger ale, and I stood to greet her.

An air kiss later and we were both in chairs on the outer deck of the restaurant. We were surrounded by white wicker tables and chairs, and beyond that, the sea. It was peaceful, beautiful, and pricey. The charm eased some of the sting of the prices, though. "I'm so glad you came."

"I almost didn't after that little display last night," she teased me but gave me some right back with the statement.

She had on a flowing, sleeveless, pink cotton dress with dark roses embroidered down one side and a pair of black sandals. Unlike me, her face was made up and her hair done properly.

"I'm surprised you could climb out of bed long

enough to come out," I teased and lifted my sunglasses to wink at her.

"Hey! That's not fair! I didn't tease you when you could barely crawl out of that room after your first night with Dylan!" She lifted her glasses to give me a wink and continued. "I totally could have teased you mercilessly, the way you were walking."

"Oh, that's just cruel!" I felt a little better as our banter continued. "I, at least, had an excuse. You've been around that block a time or two more than me."

"That's true. You're right." She shook her head and pursed her lips in a totally smug smile. "So many more times."

"You're terrible, really." She wasn't, and she knew it.

Jessi joined us a few minutes later, so the conversation moved to introductions and ordering food and drinks. I had an extra portion of Ranch dressing brought with my salad, and Jessi smirked at me. I narrowed my eyes at her, but she kept her mouth shut. Not without a very naughty wink, though.

She knew I hadn't told anyone else yet, but she was excited. I couldn't blame her. I wanted to tell Roxie, Dylan, all of them, and I would. When the time was right.

"Not feeling well, today?" Jessi prodded when the salads were brought to the table, and we'd all started to eat.

I almost choked on a portion of lettuce and glared at her.

"Not really, no." I gave her a pointed look.

"I hope you feel better soon."

"What's wrong, Emily?" Roxie asked, not immune to the nonverbal communication that had been going on.

"Nothing, just a tummy bug. I'll be fine," I lied, but I didn't like it.

"Poor thing. I shouldn't have teased you. I thought you had a hangover or something, or maybe a migraine. You'd left your sunglasses on, so I thought it must be one of those."

"No, I haven't had a migraine since—" I'd been about to say since I got pregnant but put the brakes on that. "Not in a while now."

"Good. I hated seeing you in so much pain."

We went back to eating, but before long Jessi and Roxie started to chat. Roxie told her about Elmo's, about how she'd gotten into the business, and Jessi just gaped at her.

"You were dancing at clubs when you were sixteen?" Jessi hadn't been raised in poverty, but she hadn't had rich parents. However, she had been raised in my family's house, and had been very sheltered for the longest time. Since she'd married Trent she'd seen a lot more of the world, but like me, she hadn't been exposed to the darker side of life.

"My dad ran out on my mom, and Mom became an alcoholic. I had to make money somehow. A cousin of mine told me about it, and well, here I am. Still doing it all these years later."

"You made something more out of it. That's what Emily said. She's so proud of you, you know?"

Roxie's gaze flicked to me, and I saw something like tears sparkle in her blue eyes, but she blinked them away in an instant. "I only did what I had to do. I enjoy the art of it now. In the early days, it was a nightmare. Men are such sleezebags, but I got lucky and had a group of women who protected me. They kept the worst of the men away from me and showed me the ropes."

"I'd like to see you perform," Jessi shocked me by saying, and I gaped at her. "What? Art is art, and what she does is art."

"I know, but, I just can't picture you…" I sputtered. "You aren't going with me with Dylan. I'm putting my foot down about that. Seriously, I'm not walking in that place with Trent in tow."

"No, it's not about that. I just want to appreciate what she does. I admire her ability, that's all. You really do amaze me, you know?" Jessi turned to say to Roxie, who just smiled politely.

"What do you think?" I asked my friend.

"It's fine with me. I don't have any objections. You know me, I don't make a lot of demands on anyone."

"No, you don't. I don't want you to feel like an exhibit either."

"Oh girl, stop! I'm an exhibitionist, obviously, or I wouldn't do what I do. It's not a problem. I promise. Don't worry."

"Well, if you're sure?" I knew what she'd said, but I wanted to be really sure.

"Cool it, Emily. It's fine. I'd be happy for you to bring Jessi. Your other sister-in-law, if she wants to come."

"Laura? I'm not sure it's her thing, but I'll—" I paused when Jessi waved her hand at me.

"Oh, yeah, Laura wants to come too. She's even more amazed than me."

"Really?" Roxie and I asked at the same time.

"Indeed. She's captivated by the grace of it all. I think she might start taking lessons or something. She's fascinated."

We both watched her, and she smiled. "I'm serious. She really likes it. Plus, she thinks Mason might get a kick out of it. You know she's pregnant, and older than him, and well, I think she wants a confidence boost."

"I can give her lessons. Gentle ones if she's pregnant," Roxie amended at the end, and I felt myself blanch. Roxie didn't seem to notice, though, because she was ordering another drink.

"I guess it's a plan then," I said to cover up my silence and yawned.

"You should get home and rest until you feel better, Emily," Roxie urged, but I shook my head.

"No, it's doing me some good, being out of the office and in the sunlight. I get so cold in there sometimes."

"I nearly froze to death when..." but Jessi didn't finish because I kicked her under the table. "When I was working at the resorts."

"Damn bugs are out already."

"You were cold even with the ovens?" Roxie asked, confused. She knew Jessi was a baker before she married Trent.

"Yeah, sometimes that was the only thing that kept me warm." She sipped at her drink and looked away.

I hated making her lie.

The moment sucked all of the fun out of the meeting. Jessi made it all better, though. She asked Roxie about the places she'd been to perform, and before long we were laughing all over again.

"I can't imagine the life you've had. You're really an amazing woman."

"I'm just me, Jessi, that's all I can be." It wasn't exactly a brush off of the compliment, but I knew Roxie hated them.

She was a proud woman, but she wasn't one to seek compliments. Maybe that was odd for a woman who had excelled at a profession like exotic dancing, but it was true. She hated compliments.

Jessi took off the bright green cardigan she wore and fanned her face. "It's so hot already."

"It is. The tourists are starting to stream in," Roxie pointed out.

"Traffic is going to be a nightmare soon," I remarked, and they both groaned.

"Don't remind me. I can't stand it. I think I'll have Trent send the kids and I back to Charlotte for a while," Jessi said, offhand. "Or maybe we'll find a place in the mountains."

"Now that sounds nice," Roxie said and leaned forward on the table. "Cool mountain shadows, cold springs to play in, and no tourists."

"Sounds like heaven, doesn't it?" I sighed. "Dylan needs me here, though. We're opening next week. All the stupid little things that have caused delays are sorted, and we're ready to accept guests, at last."

Which was one more thing stressing Dylan out at the moment. Those final details, but I knew there was nothing he could do about most of it. Things would go wrong and would need to be sorted that first week, but really, that was what he had staff for.

"Maybe after the opening, in a month or two, when it's really hot and super busy, you could get away?" Jessi asked, and I glanced at Roxie.

"Maybe we should all escape for a week, without the

kids or the men, and just have a vacation to ourselves? You could get Laura to come too."

"That sounds like a really good plan, actually," Roxie agreed. "I can take the time off, and it would do me good."

"Even with Nathan?" I asked, pointedly.

"It would do him good not to have me around for a week." She had that smug look again. "Remind him of what he'd be missing if he walked away."

"Absence makes the heart grow fonder," Jessi muttered, and we all laughed.

"We can talk about it more later, but I guess we need to find a place first, don't we? Everything might get booked up otherwise," I prompted, and Jessi waved me off. "I know a place. I'll call them later this afternoon."

"Good. That settles that then."

"August would be good," Roxie said, and we all agreed. Right before the kids went back to school, and the last of the tourists were catching what sun they could before the fall came along. It would do us all good to miss that.

I'd be much bigger by then, but not too big. Just big enough for it to be noticeable. I could feel this emotion like excitement mixed with something sweet and happy, and looked at my friends. "I'm so lucky."

"Fuck me, don't start crying, Emily." Roxie handed me a napkin. "I'll cry with you, at this point."

"As if you'd ever cry," I answered and wiped my nose.

"I don't know. Nathan's made me soft, I think. I cried over a movie the other night. So much ick."

"Say it isn't so?" I breathed out with mock drama.

"It is so, my dear. I couldn't believe it."

"Men make us do strange things," Jessi butted in, and I nodded.

"You're right, sister." I raised my fist in solidarity with her, and we all laughed again.

It had been a pleasant lunch, and I was sad to see it end, but Jessi had to get back to let the babysitter go home, and Roxie had to get ready for work.

I stopped Roxie as she started to leave.

"I'm glad to see you happy, honey. I really am."

"I know. It's taken a long time, but I think he might be the one for me." She put her bag down on the table and sat. "I can't wait for you to meet him."

"Oh, I get to meet him?"

"You have to. Until he gets your seal of approval, he's on shaky ground." She kissed my cheek and got up to leave. "I value your opinion, even if you aren't as experienced as me."

She flounced off with another wink then, and I couldn't help but laugh. How had these women worked so much magic on me in such a little time? Maybe it was the sea air, but I had a feeling it was them.

I went back in to work and managed to get some

work done. Dylan came in to check on me, his gait a little slower than it had been, but otherwise, you wouldn't know he'd been unable to walk at all a couple of weeks ago.

"How are you darling? I know you aren't feeling well." He pulled me into his arms and had a look at me. "You look better than you did this morning, though."

"I think lunch did me good." I deflected and kissed him to distract him.

There was one thing that hadn't changed since Dylan had become ill. Our passion hadn't dimmed at all. Even with my morning sickness and the exhaustion I felt, I still craved his body and mind. His attention.

"You distract me so easily, woman. I came in to ask if you wanted to have dinner with Laura and Mason. He called me, but I think I'll answer him later."

I was a bit surprised my brother had called him, but Dylan distracted me as soon as he closed the door to my office and backed me up against it. I could be surprised later, I decided, and wrapped my arms around his neck.

16

DYLAN

I went through a pile of work orders, invoices, and wished, for just a minute, that I'd given up on the idea of opening a new resort. I was tired, and all I wanted to do was soak in the hot tub with Emily. My back was sore, and my eyes were on fire.

It wasn't my illness, it was just exhaustion. We were about to open, only a couple of more days to go, and the rooms had all been booked already. The problem was, little things kept being brought to my attention. I wanted everything to be perfect.

I knew it wouldn't be, I wasn't naïve, but I wanted it to be as near to perfect as it could be. I had invested my own money, and my name, into this venture. My adoptive father's name too, so there was a lot of weight on my shoulders. Luckily, Emily was there for me.

She made sure I took my medicines on time, that I

ate, that I stopped to exercise, and to rest. She'd be in shortly, if I knew her. It was like she had a schedule written up somewhere, or maybe it was a sixth sense. I didn't know, I just knew she'd made all of this a lot more bearable.

She'd been quiet lately, and her stomach had given her a lot of problems too. I knew she was stressed, and it was my job to take care of her. I put the stack of papers down and called my PA.

"Have a car brought around for me. Make reservations for Emily and I at that new French place." The PA agreed happily, and I went up to get Emily.

It was after five, so I knew she'd be up in the kitchen of our penthouse. I wasn't surprised to find her there. "How about you change, and we go out for dinner? Let's blow this joint for a little while."

"Sounds like heaven. I'll be five minutes." She disappeared and true to her word, five minutes later she was back in the kitchen.

She had on a loose black silk dress that danced around her knees and a pair of flat black sandals. She looked romantic, sweet, and always sexy. "Beautiful as always, my sweet."

"Thank you." She pecked my lips, and we left the building. Dinner was a calm affair, but I was surprised at how much Ranch salad dressing she asked for. She gave me this guilty but totally unrepentant look, and I laughed.

"As long as you're happy, darling."

"I love this stuff. Can't help it." She poured the bowl into her salad, and the poor lettuce began to float. That didn't look healthy at all, but she seemed to savor each bite.

When we got home, Emily took a shower, brushed her teeth, and put on a silky sheer nightgown. I found her in the bed ready for me when I came out of the shower myself. "Mm, that looks like dessert is being served."

"It is. Come eat me all up, Dylan." Her finger enticed me to draw nearer, and so I did.

I crawled over her and pressed my hips to hers. "I hope you aren't too full."

"On the contrary, I'm starving for what you have to give me."

"Good, because I have plenty to give you." It might be silly, but my first thought when I realized my legs had stopped working that night was the fact that my dick wouldn't work if I was dead from the waist down. Then, I'd panicked about the rest, but that really had been my first thought.

Everything worked perfectly fine now, to my relief, and I nuzzled at Emily's neck with sensual kisses. I felt her shiver beneath me, and my body grew warmer. Her responses to me always made me hot.

With slow, gentle ease I moved my lips down her neck, over her collarbone, and pushed the panel of the gown away from her left breast. Something looked different there, but I couldn't decide what. Or why.

"Are your nipples darker than usual?" It wasn't really a concern, I was just confused by it.

"I don't know, are they?" She sounded as if she was holding her breath, but I had just licked her nipple.

"Doesn't matter." I took the bud between my lips and sucked at it with a deep tug. She moaned, and I felt her hips twitch against me.

I moved to the other one and made sure it was just as hard before I turned my attentions elsewhere. My need to subjugate her, once so strong within me, had settled over the last few weeks. Maybe it would come back, I didn't know, but I didn't miss it.

I'd been too busy, and Emily had shown me time after time that I didn't need to be so angry about life. She'd shown me that there was a reason to smile. I knew I'd never totally lose the urge to be dominant, it was part of who I was now, but I no longer felt like I had to punish her.

I'd reacted badly to the news about who her family was, and for a while, I'd treated her as if she'd deserved to be subjugated. I hated that about myself, but I hadn't been able to stop it. She hadn't complained, she'd taken it until I'd seen that it didn't matter how much I did, she'd take whatever I gave her. As long as she had me.

"You are too good for me, Emily," I whispered as I moved down her tummy. It was a bit round, but she'd had a lot of salad with her dinner. A rather large amount, but she blamed hormones. I hadn't questioned that and splayed my fingers over the roundness. It made me chuckle, knowing she'd eaten that much, and she squirmed.

"Don't laugh at my salad belly!" she complained, and I laughed louder.

"Darling you ate about five pounds of salad, if I'm not mistaken." My hand went lower and teased at her slit without opening her. Just enough to let her know I was there.

"I needed the nutrients, obviously. Don't tease me, Dylan, it's cruel." She wiggled in my arms and tried to force my hand deeper.

"Don't be so eager, madam. Enjoy the moment. We'll be too busy in a couple of days to do this."

"It's going to be hell, isn't it?" I heard her sigh though, just as my mouth moved along the place where my fingers had been. I gathered her moisture on my tongue and savored her flavor. It seemed different, sweeter, but I noticed her flavor sometimes changed.

"It won't be too bad," I breathed out over her skin.

"Maybe we can escape for a few trysts in between demanding guests and screaming staff."

"How many do you think will quit that first week?" Her voice shook, but she got the words out, even though my fingers had just slid inside of her to open her up.

"A few, but not many. Some of the newbies, definitely. The ones who stay will be loyal."

"Good. Now shut up and make me come please." Her fingers came down on my head and held it still while she rocked her clit against my tongue. "Fuck, that feels incredible, Dylan. Don't stop."

I obliged and made sure she was wrung dry before I found my own pleasure inside of her. Fucking Emily had always been a pleasure, but now that I knew that pleasure could be stripped away without notice, I made an effort to savor each moment.

I would hate life if I could no longer have sex, but I would hate it even more if I had to impose that on Emily. I had plans for after the opening, things I wanted to talk to her about, choices we had to talk about, and hopefully a future to plan. I wanted to do so much, but I hesitated. I knew she wouldn't complain if we couldn't have sex anymore, there was more than one way to sexual gratification, but I knew she wanted kids one day. If I couldn't give her that, and denied her sexual gratification at the same time, well, I would feel like a rather shit example of a man.

"So good," she whispered, and I kissed her hot skin.

Her legs were over my shoulders, and I was on my knees, blissful as I slid into her over and over again. This was heaven, and I never wanted it to end. I felt her hand slide between our bodies, and my greedy little imp gasped as she found that spot that made her shiver so beautifully.

She took herself on another ride to the land of nothing, and this time I followed along behind her. I experienced each moment with a sense of wonder, afraid that it might be the last time and I'd forget what it had been like. Ever since that night, every moment with Emily was like that, but when I was inside of her, I made sure I memorized every second of the experience. I never wanted to forget what it felt like.

She rolled away when I moved off of her and caught her breath. She wasn't turning away from me, just having a moment to recover. I sighed and let my eyes close. I heard her go into the bathroom and then come out a few minutes later.

"Good night, Dylan." She kissed me, and I tasted toothpaste on her lips.

"Good night, Emily." I pulled her to me, and she curled into my side, her head on my chest. I held her there and stared at the ceiling now that the light was off.

Thoughts ran around in my head. Plans I had and the things we wanted to do together. So far, the new medicine was working, and I wanted to make sure I took advantage of each day. I'd spent so much time dreading the moment when I might have a flare, when Emily would know what was wrong with me, that I felt as if I'd barely lived our lives together.

I'd only been half invested, but now, I wanted to be fully invested in whatever we planned to do in the future. I was even considering a wedding, at some point. In the future.

I frowned, but I knew it was a big step. I was certain Emily was the one for me, the one I wanted to spend my life with, such as it may be, but I wasn't sure if it was too soon. She wasn't the kind to watch romantic movies, or stare at wedding magazines; she'd never even mentioned it, so maybe she didn't want to get married?

I knew she wasn't an assuming person, and she wouldn't push for anything she thought I didn't want, but I did wonder sometimes. She never, ever mentioned marriage, at all. Not even by accident.

It was a possibility, then, that she didn't want to marry anyone.

She'd seen the kind of marriage her parents had, and although it was nothing like my parents, her parents weren't exactly the most loving or warm people to their children. From what I'd seen so far, they weren't that way with each other either.

Maybe she wanted to avoid it? Which would be fine,

I wouldn't push her if she didn't want it, but I would like to give her that protection, in case something happened to me. I wanted to know that she'd be taken care of.

Of course, she had family who would always do that, I suspected now that they'd got over their squabble. I hadn't completely thawed to Trent, but I liked Kevin and Mason. They were intelligent fellas and not as unyielding as Trent. We'd had dinner with Laura and Mason the other night. They'd seemed like good company, and Emily was happy to be with them.

She'd been distracted, but she had been that way since I'd fallen ill. I knew she was probably calculating when I had to take my medicine next, or if I'd been still too long. She caught my gaze on her and smiled. She was alright, but I was worried that she was dealing with too much stress.

I'd take her for a weekend away, I decided. After the opening and everything had settled down. I knew she had a girls' weekend planned with Roxie and her sisters-in-law, but that was later this summer. She deserved a couple of days before then, at least.

I knew she was exhausted, but she'd stayed that way lately. She was already snoring softly against my shoulder. I shifted a little, and her head moved. The snores stopped, but she was still asleep. The poor thing couldn't get enough sleep lately. I'd make sure she slept in the next morning. One way or another.

I slid out from beneath her and went to her phone. I turned off the alarm she'd set and crawled back into bed. She curled into me and I sighed, happy to have her by my side.

I wouldn't have believed it when I first met her, but even then, I'd known there was something different about her. How right I'd been. She was different from any woman I'd ever met, and that was what made her special.

I thought about the next day and all I had to get done. It all stopped mattering when Emily made a soft sound of fear in her sleep. I soothed her, and she fell back into something more peaceful.

I watched her sleep for a while longer, and I didn't even realize I'd fallen asleep until Emily moved away, and that woke me up. I patted her back and rolled to my side, too tired to fight it anymore.

I'd make sure she took care of herself tomorrow, and that we'd both get some sleep tonight. I let the dreams take me, at last, and started to snore.

The next morning, Emily wasn't in bed. I was disappointed to find she had got up already, and I got up to find her. "Emily? Why are you up, darling? I turned your alarm off, woman!"

I heard noises in the bathroom and went to the door. "Emily?"

"Don't come in! I must have eaten something bad last night."

I could hear she'd been crying, and I didn't want to invade her privacy, but she needed me. "Emily? I think we should take you to the doctor, sweetheart. You've been ill a lot lately, and I'm worried about you."

"I don't need to go to the doctor, Dylan. I know what's wrong." I heard the toilet flush and the door opened. "Let's go to the kitchen, and I'll explain it all."

Her face was drained of all color and her eyes were terrified, but she walked to the kitchen with a determined gait. I wasn't sure what she was about to tell me, but I suspected it was something important.

17

DYLAN

 watched as Emily poured herself a glass of ginger ale from the fridge and came to stand in front of me on the other side of the island. She looked rough, worn out, and pale. I didn't like the look of her and wanted to ask her to let me take her to the doctor, but she brushed her hair back from her face, took a deep breath, and looked me straight in the eye.

"I'm pregnant." Her mouth was a grim straight line, and her eyes lacked their normal sparkle, but as soon as she said the words, I knew they were true. Maybe I'd never been around pregnant women, and I didn't really know the first thing about pregnancy, but it all made sense now.

The stomach nausea, the exhaustion, the paleness, even the way her nipples had darkened, all made sense now. She was pregnant. I could only stare at her and nod.

"Alright. Well, that's good I suppose." I sat there, too stunned to ask her how, or why, or what should we do. A baby.

A few months ago, I'd have coldly told her to abort it, and then I'd have dumped her. Now? I wasn't sure what I felt, but coldness wasn't the name for it. I wasn't angry, I wasn't sad, I was just … numb.

"Good?" she said, her eyes disappointed.

I couldn't help it, though. This was a big thing, on top of so many big things, and well, I was fucked if I could think of how to respond. I knew I should be angry or excited, one of the two, but right now, I just wanted to process the whole thing. I wasn't always able to handle surprises well, and this was one of those times.

This was one major surprise.

"When, er, how long until it's born?" That was one of the things you were supposed to ask, right?

"Seven months or so. Give or take a week." She sat on the bar stool and took a deep breath. Her eyes had been on her glass of ginger ale, but now she looked up at me, hurt in the gray depths I loved so much. "Look, I know this might be more than you can handle right now, but I can't hide it anymore."

She took a sip of the soda and continued.

"I wanted to wait until the time was right, until the

perfect moment, but I can't keep trying to hide how sick I am. Or the cravings. Or how my body has started to change already."

"That explains the Ranch dressing then. I knew you wouldn't normally eat that much. The tuna, you hate tuna."

"I do. If you can't accept this, and you don't want anything else to do with me I understand. This wasn't supposed to happen. Apparently, my birth control failed because of the migraine medicine, and well, it's real now. I don't want to change that, or us, but if you don't want to be part of this, then I understand, Dylan. You have a lot on your plate."

"What? No, Emily. Come here." I held my arms out, and she immediately burst into tears as she fell into my embrace. "Darling, no, don't cry."

"It's not your fault. It seems to be my default response lately. The sky is a wonderful shade of blue, I cry. I'm happy about a new employee, I cry. You don't kick me out and accept what's happened, I cry." She sniffled her way through the words, but she got them out, her head against my shoulder.

"It's alright, Emily. I'll take care of you. You did it for me, and it's my turn now." I kissed the top of her head and pulled away slightly. "Are you going to be alright if I head in to work?"

She blinked at me, a little blankly, and I knew I'd

failed her again. She'd hoped for an emotional response on either side of the spectrum, and I'd landed square in the middle of both sides. I wasn't angry, but I wasn't excited either.

"Yeah, sure, go ahead. I've got some calls to make anyway." She swiped her hand across her face and then went to get a paper towel.

I headed for the shower, my brain just barely on tickover. I was still completely dumbfounded when I found myself in my office an hour later. How was I going to raise a child, if I was dead?

The question played on repeat in my head, and I finally pushed my desk chair away to stare out of the large pane of glass behind me. I stared down at the work going on below, at the ocean beyond, and saw that a storm was rolling in.

I imagined there was one rolling in upstairs too. I hadn't responded well to Emily's announcement, but I couldn't fake emotions I didn't have. Not very well at least. The moment she'd said those words everything in my brain froze, and I couldn't help but sit there, totally stumped.

I'd have to make it up to her somehow.

I wasn't sure what that 'how' was, or if I could accomplish anything that would put her at ease, but I'd try.

A baby. My baby.

Something warm started to glow in my chest, and I could feel a smile spread over my face. Emily was pregnant with my baby. It wasn't so bad. In fact, as the day went on, that warmth spread, and everything about the day somehow became easier. It wasn't so stressful when a pipe burst in a bathroom on the second floor and flooded the room below. When the maintenance guys found one of the brand-new mowers had been stolen, well, no big deal, I'd just buy a new one.

The entire day went like that and by the time I closed my office door for the day, I had a plan in place. I drove myself out to a boutique on the outskirts of town, bought Emily a cap-sleeved, calf-length maternity dress of black silk with an empire waist that was sexy but formal. I also bought a few baby clothes, tiny little things that I had to stare at for a while. It hit me then, how much this baby would depend on us and how we'd have to be so careful with it.

A tiny little life that would depend on us for every ounce of sustenance, care, and love that we could possibly give it. I would be a father, as my real father and my adoptive father had been. It would be my job to make sure this baby was loved and grew up as a functioning adult. Fuck.

I nearly had to sit down but stayed on my feet. This was huge.

So huge.

I stared around the shop, an expensive place with labels that most people didn't know about, but the rich coveted entirely. I didn't want my child to be like the people I knew, so far up their own asses that most of them couldn't see the real world around them. Or cloistered away like Emily had been, unloved, forgotten, and expendable, until she'd stood up for herself.

I wanted our baby to have a puppy and a home without show-room living spaces, I wanted to have crayons on the floor and fingerprints on the walls. I wanted the life my real father had wanted and tried to give me. Somehow, I knew Emily would want the same thing.

She'd never said she wanted a dog, but I stopped at the local animal shelter anyway. I found a delightful little fella named Corky, a chihuahua and dachshund mix, and started the adoption process. It would take a few days, but I didn't mind. I had his picture and a letter that gave his details. I then stopped at a florist and ordered so many flowers I could barely fit them into the car, along with a pile of balloons.

I was on the verge of laughing out loud when the security guard saw me drive in. He looked astonished, and when I asked him to have someone come down and help me, his jaw nearly dropped. I did laugh out loud then.

Together, we managed to carry everything up. I'd

had the clothes gift wrapped, and the boxes were in my hands when Emily opened the door at my knock. I couldn't open the blasted thing without dropping boxes or flowers everywhere, so I'd had to knock.

"Dylan?" She looked surprised, which is what I wanted. "What's all this?"

She'd seen the guy behind me then.

"This is the reaction I should have given you this morning, my dear. Come along, into the living room." I marched her and the guy behind me in, tipped the man after he'd set everything down, and watched her as he let himself out of our home.

"What is all of this, Dylan? Really?" She had tears in her eyes again, but they were happy tears, so it was alright.

"Here, open this one first." I handed her the box that I knew had the dress in it and sat down beside of her.

The living room was now filled with roses, carnations, tulips, and a variety of other flowers, as well as the stack of boxes.

"Oh, it's beautiful, Dylan." She pulled the dress out of the box and held it up. It was a light, stretchy material that would suit her well as her belly grew.

"I know you'll probably have a dozen more dresses by the time this is finished, but I wanted to get you one too. And these."

I handed her the much lighter boxes and felt delight as her eyes went round. "Baby clothes?"

"I got them in neutral colors, until we know what we're having. I just wanted you to know, I'm in this with you. You aren't alone and won't have to be. As long as we can keep me healthy, that is."

"It's a good reason to stay healthy, don't you think?" she asked and opened another box. It was mainly sleepwear and onsies, and I'd even found the tiniest pair of socks that I couldn't resist buying. "I think you've got the baby's entire wardrobe for the first year of its life here."

"Oh, the saleswoman told me that I'd need to get clothes in a variety of different sizes, because the baby would grow so much in its first year."

"She's right." Emily leaned over to kiss me on the cheek and stayed there. "You've done well, Dylan. This is fantastic."

"I hope so. I know I didn't give you what you wanted this morning, but I'm not totally stumped now. I'm sorry, I hope I didn't upset you too much."

"I was a little disappointed, but it was a shock. You have a lot on your plate, Dylan. A lot. I knew it wouldn't be easy for you."

"You always think about me before you, don't you, Emily? It always amazes me just how thoughtful you are."

"Just wait until this baby is born; you're going to have to be almost as thoughtful as me."

"I can only try to do my best." I chuckled and moved. "Oh, there's this too."

I found the piece of paper in the folder, lost amongst wrapping paper and boxes. "This might be the most important part of all."

"What is it?" she asked and opened the folder. "You're kidding me?"

Her head whipped back to look at me, and I knew I'd done really well.

"You like him?"

"I've always wanted a dog! I almost got one when I first met you, but I didn't want to neglect it by leaving it at my place so much. I didn't know if you'd want one."

"I always wanted one, but my real mother was a little nuts, and we were afraid to have one in the house. My adoptive mother is allergic to dogs, somehow. So I never had one. I thought our little one should grow up knowing what puppy love is."

"He's perfect." She stared at the picture of the dog with large brown eyes and a curious look on his face. "I love him already."

"I'm not so sure about his name."

"Oh, his name is fine, Dylan. Let's not confuse him by changing it."

"You're right." I leaned back on the couch, relaxed

now that I knew she was happy. "So what do you think we should name the baby?"

"Caroline, if it's a girl, because of the place where we met. Or Charles for a boy?" she offered, and I knew she'd been thinking on it.

"Or we could call it Charlie, either way." I liked the sound of it, even if it wasn't a conventional name anymore. I liked her idea of naming the baby for where we'd met and fell in love. I hadn't told her that part yet, but I would when the time was right.

"I like Caroline better if it's a girl, and you could call her Charlie," she offered, a light tease in her eyes.

"I like Charlie," I grumped and looked away, teasing her back. "You're her mother. So if you prefer Caroline, then that's what her name shall be."

"We can call her Charlie. Or him." She laughed and gave in, as I knew she would.

"No, she'll be called Caroline. That's your choice, my dear, and I can't take it from you."

"Thank you, Dylan. You've just made the day so much better with this. Thank you."

"Good. I felt terrible about how I'd left you this morning. You were vulnerable, and I just left you standing there. It wasn't very good of me, but then, I'm not very good at this relationship stuff, as you know."

"You're doing just fine, Dylan, don't worry." She

stretched, yawned, and looked over at me. "Shall we go to bed?"

"If you're tired, my dear, then you should rest." I stood, ready to usher her into the bedroom. I'd found this new side of me, that was caring and helpful, now that I knew she was going to have my baby.

"I didn't say I wanted to sleep, Dylan. I asked if you wanted to go to bed." That glint was in her eye, and I couldn't help the response my body gave immediately.

"As you wish, my dear."

18

EMILY

"I can't believe we lived through that," I said as Dylan put the car into drive and drove us away from the resort. At this point, a week after the grand opening, I didn't care if I ever saw the place again.

"I've dealt with irate customers, angry workers, and mishaps beyond belief my entire life, but that city councilman's wife finding him in bed with a prostitute might have taken the cake."

"I just knew the reporters would show up at any minute while you were picking this up." I relaxed into the heated seat of the Audi e-tron, a family car, as Dylan had put it. It was a hybrid car, and he really loved it so far. So did I.

I looked at all the bells and whistles as he drove toward Elmo's, a night of fun and relaxation planned after a most tumultuous week. "What's this one do?"

I poked at one of the buttons, and the sound came on. "I think that's the radio, but I'm not sure."

"At least we've managed to escape for a while. I've told them not to call us for anything. We need some time away from that place," Dylan said and reached over to pat my hand. "You deserve some time off."

"I think I'll be taking plenty of time off soon enough, but you're right. A night away from the resort sounds heavenly."

We arrived at Elmo's soon enough, and Dylan led me into the place with his arm at the small of my back. I had on that lovely dress he'd bought me to make up for his less than stellar reaction to my announcement, paired up with a pair of flat sandals. I didn't care what duchesses across the ocean did while they were pregnant, I wasn't wearing another pair of heels until this baby was born.

I was far too clumsy to let society dictate to me what I would and wouldn't wear while I carried a life inside of me. I also didn't mind that I was so much shorter than Dylan. It made me feel like he was my protector when I subtracted the inches that heels gave me. Of course, he always felt like that to me, which was one of the reasons I loved the man so much.

I thought about his reaction when I sat at a table in the bar area. Roxie was on stage, and her performance was mesmerizing as always, but I couldn't take my eyes off of Dylan. He'd been so floored by my news that I didn't think it actually sank in until a few hours later.

I'd been aware that he might react strangely and hadn't been too upset when he'd carried on with his day. A little excitement might have been nice, but when he came home with all those gifts, and the image of the puppy, I couldn't have asked for more, really. Corky was now happy behind the front reception desk with two very happy young women to lavish attention on him, happy as a king from the looks of him when we'd left.

That had taken some getting used to, having a new life to take care of, and he'd given every bit of care back with a hundred times the love. He liked the women who ran the front desk at night, so he was happy to stay there, but he'd be happy when we picked him up later.

"Penny for your thoughts," Dylan said softly as he sat with two glasses. One had a small amount of scotch in it, and the other my now ever-present ginger ale. It was all I wanted to drink.

"I was just thinking about Corky."

"He's something, isn't he? A little handful of love." Dylan relaxed into his chair and put his legs under the table. "I'm glad we got him."

"I'm glad you got him too." He'd already broken the rules by jumping into bed with me. He'd curl up against my stomach until I fell asleep, then he'd wiggle down to curl up behind my legs. It made me smile, even if it wasn't the best thing to do.

"At least he's house trained," I added.

Dylan looked up, and his face changed; a look of confusion changed to curiosity. "Is that Trent walking out?"

He pointed to somewhere behind me, and I turned to look but couldn't see anyone. "I missed him. I don't know why he'd be here, though. Jessi wants to come, but she promised she'd come with me first."

"I guess it wasn't him." Dylan didn't look exactly convinced, and his demeanor had changed. "I'm still not sure if I trust him, but I try for you."

"That's all you can do, really, darling. He did a lot to try to damage you here, and the stuff with me … well, it's best we put it away, but I understand why you can't get over it."

"You're right. It's time to let it go. Besides, I have a very beautiful woman here with me, an equally beautiful woman dancing on stage, and a peaceful night ahead of me. If you choose to keep it peaceful."

I liked the way he teased me and grinned at him. "I'll keep it in mind."

I had slowed down a little in the sex department, but not by much. Something about being pregnant kept me constantly in the mood, though, even if I was always too tired to be as adventurous as I normally was. I stroked his hand and watched Roxie perform.

When she finished, she joined us at our table in the dimly lit room that was only a small part of the larger facility that was Elmo's.

"How are you guys? It's great to see you!" She sat across from me after a peck on the cheek and looked at us. "What's up?"

"We have news," I answered and waited for her to respond.

"Oh, and what's that, Queen of Mystery?" She gave me that smug look she sometimes had on, and I had a feeling I wasn't about to surprise her at all.

"I'm going to have a baby," I announced without fanfare and waited.

"I thought so. Congratulations!" She leaned over, happy and excited, despite her intuition. "That's just perfect. Really, I'm so happy for you."

She squeezed my hand then gave Dylan a kiss on his cheek too. "Good for you, sticking around and being a man. Not a lot of men do that anymore, it would seem."

"I wouldn't miss this for the world."

I gasped at his response, and I knew that somehow this baby would finish the healing that Dylan needed to get on with his life. He would give it all the love he was denied, and to me, that was perfect.

"Good. Now, there's a new girl coming on that you

might want to watch. I found her in a club not far from here. She's very beautiful, and almost has my skills." She had on a smirk that made me giggle.

"We'll watch her then. Oh, can I talk to you for a minute?" I said as she made to stand up.

"Sure, you can come back with me while I change. What's up?" She blew Dylan a kiss goodbye, and I followed her to her dressing room.

"Nothing, I just wanted to find out if you were still on for that trip to the mountains. Jessi has it scheduled for the middle of August. We thought you might need to ask for time off."

"I do, and that's the perfect time. I won't miss the money I'll lose being gone for a week, because, um, Nathan's moving in with me." She had an expectant look on her face, and I squealed with happiness for her.

"Oh my goodness, Roxie! Are you serious? I'm so happy for you."

"You're pregnant, that's so much better!" She did her own bout of girlish laughter as we hugged and bounced gently together.

"It's great, but you have love! I'm, fuck, I'm so excited for you!" I hugged her tight around her neck, and we were both talking over each other when I felt something. A rumble beneath our feet, followed quickly by a boom and the smell of smoke. "What the hell was that?"

I froze in fear, and Roxie did the same thing. "I don't

know what the fuck that was, but it can't be good. Come on, let's get you out of here."

"Put some clothes on first! We have to leave the building, and you can't go outside in that; you'll be arrested!" She only wore a robe covering her stage costume. She kicked off her heels, put on a pair of jeans over the thong, and threw on a t-shirt over the glitzy bra she had on. I started to cough as smoke filled her room, and she reached for me. The power went off in the building just as she slid her feet into a pair of flip flops, grabbed my hand, and pulled me out of the room.

"Put this over your mouth and try to breathe through it." She handed me a tablecloth she'd grabbed from one of the tables, and she did the same thing. I could barely stop coughing, even with the cloth over my face, but I reached up to tie it in place. I needed my hands to stay upright.

We pushed forward, out of the stage area, and into the bar until we were close to the right wall leading out to the entryway. I'd heard the sounds of mayhem outside her door, but I'd tried to ignore it as she quickly got dressed. Now, the screams and sounds of running feet were hard to ignore. Screams filled the air, and some loud, shrill, beeping noise added to the den inside the small bar. That must be the fire alarm, I thought stupidly as my feet stumbled, and I fell into a woman in front of me.

People rushed around us, screaming words that we couldn't hear, but I didn't hear Dylan's voice. I tried to look for him in the small bar area, but it had filled with young adults from the dance club portion of the place. They were everywhere and blocked most of my view as we slowly moved forward, one body length at a time. I felt parts of people I never wanted to feel on strangers as I fought to stay standing up. Roxie was behind me, and she pushed at anybody who got close to me, if she could. Her hands were planted on my waist, and I was thankful to have that support. Chaos erupted further when another explosion rocked the back end of the building. I tensed and tried not to add to the screams that reached a new peak of intensity.

I'd fought the urge to scream for Dylan in the smoke-filled air. I knew he wouldn't be able to find me, and I hoped he was already outside. I hadn't seen him in the bar area, but then, the place was full of smoke. When the explosion rocked the building, I tried to scream for Roxie but couldn't because my lungs were on fire and gasping for fresh air. I screamed her name harshly through a throat that felt as if it was on fire, as the crowd behind me surged forward.

I was knocked to the ground, torn away from Roxie's supporting hands, and I hit my head on something hard and solid. At first, the noise disappeared, and everything was quiet. I instinctively wrapped my arms around my stomach protectively and curled into a ball. I felt as if time had slowed down around me, and my brain screamed at me to protect the baby. I tried to avoid the feet that tripped over me and the hands that caught at my body as those that fell stood back up. I tried to flatten myself against the wall, but that didn't help as bodies streamed by, and I wondered, stupidly, how many others had fallen.

It was utter madness, and all I could do was wait there for my chance to get up and get out of the place. The air was cleaner down here, though it still stank of smoke, and I inhaled it with greed. I shut my eyes and tried to remain calm, but I could feel the wetness of tears on my face, and I started to feel dizzy.

The world began to swirl around, and I fought to stay conscious. Another foot, not as big and with less force, banged my head against the wall again like a racket ball, and a buzzing started in my ears. I whimpered out a sound of pain, of fear, and tried to call out for Roxie again. For a moment, I thought I heard Roxie screaming my name, but it was carried away as the crowd rushed like rampaging bulls to get out of the burning building. I tried to sit up, but the pain in my head increased, and nausea made me stop.

I brought my hand up as the crowd started to thin and felt something wet dripping down my hair. I felt pain in a hundred places, and my head throbbed, as if I was still being kicked. I tried to right myself again, and I pushed up from the floor, but the world tilted on its axis, and I fell over, unable to fight off the swarm in my head.

I couldn't get up, and I didn't know how much longer I could stay awake. I had to get out of the building. I couldn't stay here. It was on fire. Even down here on the floor, the space was starting to fill with smoke. I tried to crawl, I tried to call out for help again, but my parched throat wouldn't make a sound beyond an awful noise that wasn't words at all. Every move I made ended up with my head swimming, and soon, the need to stop to breathe became my only thought as smoke bloomed over and over again.

I'd wait for Dylan, I told myself. Dylan would find me. He wouldn't leave me in here to die, I knew he won't. I cradled my hands around my stomach and spoke to the baby there.

"Your daddy will save us, sweetheart. If he can find us, he'll save us."

19

DYLAN

The night was supposed to be peaceful, relaxed, and maybe sensual. I'd brought her here to celebrate the fact that we'd made it through our first week as resort operators, as puppy parents, and as a couple with a baby on the way. The flashing lights of firetrucks and police cars, the screams and mayhem, the smoke, and the fire hadn't been what I expected to be stuck in.

Yet there I was, without Emily. I'd tried to push my way back in when a stampede of people pushed me out of the bar, but a group of people held me back. When the firetrucks showed up, I slipped back inside. Most of the people were out by then, and the air had started to clear.

I knew the first firemen inside had pulled out several people, but none of them had been Emily. I'd checked every single one to make sure. I hunkered down to the floor, the air was much better down there. Now that the firemen had put some of the fire out, the air had started to clear. I still found it hard to see, and sound was strange in the midst of the noise that still prevailed.

"Emily? Roxie? Are you in here?" I called out, hoping I'd hear at least one of them call back to me. Neither one responded, though, and I kept moving.

I slid along the wall, knocked over a few potted plants that had once lined both sides of the walls, and turned when I thought I was near the bar. I'd slid along the right side of the wall going into the bar, but then I wondered if she'd have been on the right. I looked behind me, but the area was hazy again. I turned around and hoped against hope that she was still in Roxie's dressing room.

I pushed away from the wall and made my way to the room. The power was off, so I used my phone's flashlight app to look around. "Emily? Roxie? Anybody? Is there anybody in here?"

I looked around as I left the room and tried to figure out where she might have gone. I tried to retrace her steps and figured out that if she'd been swarmed by that horde of people that had flooded out of the rooms and the dance club, then she'd have probably ended up by the bar, then against that wall there. What had been on my left was now my right, and I fumbled along that area.

I even went back to look behind the bar, but she wasn't there either.

"Hey, you need to go outside, partner. Can't have people running around in here. The exit's this way." A woman in a protective suit came up to me, and I thanked the firefighter, but I told her I was looking for someone.

"That might be, but everyone who was in this area has been cleared out. We've almost got the fire under control in the back there, and I'd really appreciate it if you let me get on with my job and leave, sir." Her face was hot and damp behind her facemask, and I could see she wasn't about to budge, even if she barely came up to my chin.

"Fine. Everyone from this section was taken out you said?" I turned to follow her out, and she nodded that giant helmet that must have weighed a ton.

"Yep, if they were incapacitated, we took them to the ambulances over behind the firetrucks. You can ask about them over there."

"Thanks." I walked away, the world suddenly very dark, and not just because the moon had hidden behind some clouds. What if something had happened to her, and I hadn't protected her.

"Dylan, is that you?" A man's voice stopped me, and I turned to find Trent behind me. "Where the fuck is Emily if you're here?"

"You fucking bastard, you caused this, didn't you?" I rushed up to deck him, but he deflected the punch.

"What the fuck, Dylan? Where's Emily?"

"As if you didn't know. You did this, didn't you? You caused the fire to break Emily and I up, didn't you?" It sounded insane, even to me, but I couldn't stop the words that streamed out of my mouth. It made sense in the moment, and I didn't care who heard it.

"Look, Dylan, I mean this as politely as I can, but you're fucking insane. Why would you say that out loud while people are busy investigating what just happened? Emily told Jessi about the place and talked me into bringing her here tonight. I didn't even know you two would be here. Which leaves me with one final question, you utter dolt. Where the fuck is Emily?" Trent had stepped closer to me with each step, and his voice had dropped lower; the threat was definite. I could see it in his eyes but didn't back down.

"I apologize, but you can back the fuck off, Trent. I'm not threatened by you."

"If we don't find my sister alive, then you might want to rethink that," he growled but stepped away.

"If you two morons are done checking your dick size, I might be able to help you." I turned and gaped at Trent's wife, Jessi.

"What? Do you know where she is?" Trent turned around, his countenance completely different when he spotted his wife. It was like watching a dog's heckles suddenly flatten out.

I had been on the verge of telling Trent that if Emily wasn't found, or something had happened to her, he wouldn't have to do a damn thing to me. I'd have taken care of that all on my own.

Jessi made a motion to us, and we followed her. I didn't notice the blood red dress she had on, or how stunning she looked, all I could do was look for Emily in the faces of the crowd, until I spotted her at last. She was on a gurney, waiting on an empty ambulance to come back and take her to the hospital.

"Emily!" I ran to her, knocked Trent out of my way, which I'd admit later was childish, but I didn't care at that moment. I saw her face, covered in an oxygen mask with blood all over her.

"What's wrong with her?" I gasped out as a para-medic looked her over.

"Laceration to the scalp, multiple contusions, injuries spread along her body, smoke inhalation, and I suspect she might have more injuries that we can't see." The woman, dressed in combat pants and a button up shirt, with her last name, "Moore", stitched across the left breast, said to me, "Are you the next of kin? We're going to need them, more than likely."

"I'm her boyfriend…" I stopped when she began to shake her head no.

"We need next of kin, honey. That isn't enough."

I wanted to tell her to fuck off, but Trent stepped up and took over. He gave the information needed and promised to get the rest. Emily hadn't taken her bag in, so I knew all of her information was still in the car. I'd get that later.

"Give me your keys; I'll get her purse," Trent said when I explained where her bag was. The paramedic wanted Emily's insurance information.

I handed the keys to Emily's brother and looked down at the mother of my child.

"The baby? How's the baby?"

"The *what?*" Trent was suddenly back and glaring at me fiercely.

"She's pregnant. With my baby. Your niece or nephew."

"Fuck. I hope she's okay then." His face blanched, and fear crept across his face. "Well, I mean, I want her to be okay anyway, but if she's pregnant too, fuck, this is bad."

That didn't help my situation, but I didn't say anything else. I just stood there, looking down at the beautiful woman I wanted to wake up. She wouldn't, though, no matter how I stroked blood and soot away from her face. She was still, almost lifeless.

Another ambulance arrived then, and she was rushed into the back of the vehicle. Trent had made it back in time to hand over her insurance card and gave me back the keys.

"Which hospital is she going to?" I called into the back of the ambulance, and when the paramedic called back, I looked over at Trent.

"Meet you there?"

"You know it, brother." In an instant, the enmity fell away, and I was part of the family. "You want me to drive you?"

"That might be best. My hands are shaking."

I didn't want to admit it, but I was terrified.

"No problem. I'll have Jessi drive your car over. That shaking from stress or the other?"

Trent didn't have to say what the other was. We both knew what he meant.

"Stress, man. Look, I'll ask your dad later, but you're the de facto head of this family since your dad retired, so I'll ask you. May I marry your sister?"

He nearly drove us off the road, but he soon corrected and had us right behind the ambulance Emily was in again. "Of course. If that's what she wants."

"I don't know. We haven't talked about it. But, this?" I held my hands out in the direction of the ambulance. "If she survives this, then that's what I hope to do. Make her my wife and build a life with her."

"It's a tough decision to reach for men like us." Trent nodded, and I could hear him sigh. "I fought against my feelings for Jessi for decades, man. I know what it's like. But if you love my sister, then I'm happy to give me blessing. You should still ask my dad, though."

He winked over at me and refocused on the road.

The hospital was just as chaotic as the place we'd just left. People in medical uniforms rushed around, while people waited in the waiting area. Gurneys were pushed into an open waiting area, and I saw nothing but madness. After a minute, I started to see some direction in that chaos, and a doctor soon came to check Emily over.

"Right, get her down to radiology. Get a line running, what are her vitals?" The doctor paused while a nurse called the numbers out. "Alright. Radiology, now."

He stopped and looked up at Trent and me, a short elderly man with a shock of white hair, dressed in blue scrubs. His green eyes were bright, observant, and capable looking as he started to ask questions.

"What happened to her? I heard there was a stampede at that place. Was she involved in that? From the multiple contusions and the injuries along her body, I'd guess that's what happened."

"I don't know, she wasn't with me when the explosions started. She was with her friend."

Roxie. I'd forgotten about Roxie. I wasn't about to leave Emily's side, however. "Trent, can you get somebody to find out about Roxie? I know she's your sister, man, but I just can't leave her."

"You bet. I'll step outside for a minute."

"Okay, I need to check others while we get some tests done on her. Oh, and the baby appears to be fine right now, sir."

"Good." I felt relief flood through me, but then noticed he'd said, 'for now'. She wasn't totally out of the woods in that department then.

Hours later the stream of victims had slowed, and people had either been treated or sent home, or admitted like Emily had. She had woken up, to our relief, but she'd soon fallen asleep again. There wasn't much they could give her for the pain. Her body was covered in painful bruises that would be deep purple before it was over, and she'd needed stitches in her head, but there were no fractures, as the doctor had feared, and little Caroline/Charlie was doing just fine.

"Dylan? The baby?" she asked when she woke up, her eyes full of tears. "How's the baby?"

"It's fine, Emily. You just rest, darling. All is well." The beautiful eyes I loved more than any others in the world closed and slept again in seconds.

I faced her mom and dad, both in the room with us.

"It might not be the right time for this, but I want to ask her as soon as she wakes up. May I have your permission to marry your daughter?"

"Well, now, you're Emily's first boyfriend I think…" Her father started, but his younger bride hushed him up quickly, on the other side of her bed.

"Hush now, honey. This is what Emily needs, what she wants, and you'd be a fool to deny her that. In fact, here … I want you to use my engagement ring, please. She always loved to play with it when she was a little girl, and it's only right she has it now."

I looked down at the chunk of diamond she handed me and blinked. It was far from a cheap diamond and would have been gaudy if it hadn't been so beautiful. A little bit like Emily's mom, I guessed. The woman had on a bright blue sheath dress, and her hair and makeup were impeccable, even at this time of night.

I nodded and ducked my face away. At least they hadn't mentioned the fact that I'd had Emily at a sex club masquerading as a strip club. They were grownups, and so were we, so nobody mentioned it.

Jessi came in with Roxie a little while later. She'd spent hours looking for Emily and when Jessi found her, she'd been inconsolable, or so Jessi told me later. "Emily?"

Her voice shook as she came in, and I moved away to let her stand next to Emily. "Baby, oh please wake up and tell me you're okay."

"I'm fine, Roxie. Did you bring me ginger ale?" Emily said, sleepily, and I laughed.

"Girl, I've spent hours looking for you! You'd better wake up and tell me you're okay, properly!" Roxie's tears fell on the pale skin of Emily's hand, clenched in her own.

"What?" Emily opened her eyes and looked up at us all. "What's going on? Why are you all in my bedroom?"

"Because you're in the hospital, darling, not the bed at home." I stood closer, next to Roxie, and looked down at her. "If you wouldn't mind, would you give me the honor of marrying me?"

Everybody in the room, except for Emily and I, laughed at my outburst. I didn't care if they thought it was funny or not. All I could see was her surprise and the happiness in her eyes when she said yes.

20

EMILY

"My God, Emily. It's gorgeous," Roxie breathed the words as I turned around, my wedding dress on full display.

"Thank you." I looked at the long sheath I now had on and beamed. It was sexy, but innocent, perfect for me. It fit me perfectly.

"I can't believe this," Mom said, and I turned to her to see tears in her eyes.

"Mom? Why are you crying?"

"Because my little girl is getting married, silly; why else would I be crying? You're beautiful baby." She held Caroline, my daughter in her arms, a far cry from the woman I'd grown up with. After my trip to the hospital both of my parents had suddenly decided that they needed to be in my life far more.

They'd helped me while I was pregnant and were

always on hand to act as grandparents to my sweet little three-month-old daughter.

"Why did you wait so long to get married?" Jessi asked, and I turned to her.

"I wanted Caroline here, and then, I needed to lose the baby weight. It didn't matter to Dylan, but I knew we'd have to look at those pictures forever, so I waited." Dylan would have married me before we even left the hospital that night, but I'd wanted to have Caroline in the pictures; I wanted her to be part of the whole thing. She was a product of what led to our wedding, after all.

"I love you, gorgeous." I could barely lean over but managed to place a kiss on top of her head. When I stood, I looked at the group of women around me. "Are we ready?"

"Yes, it's time," Roxie spoke up. "Let me get your train."

It wasn't very long, but I knew she was happy to be the maid of honor.

The Galia Lahav gown had cap sleeves and was a high-necked mermaid dress that I wanted to spend the rest of my life in. It showed off every curve perfectly, and the chapel train was perfect for the outdoor wedding we'd planned at the edge of the beach of Dylan's Myrtle Beach resort. The dress was decorated with lace and had strategic panels cutout, but it wasn't gaudy; it was just sparkly and glistening goodness that I absolutely adored.

I marched down the red carpet set up outside, my dad on one side, and Trent on the other, despite convention. I'd wanted them both to give me away, and they'd agreed. I barely noticed the two hundred white chairs that fell away behind me, or the people in them; I just saw Dylan, in a soft, dark gray tux, and Roxie by his side with Caroline in his arms. Mason stood in as his best man, since Trent had walked me down the aisle, and I saw Laura beaming with pride on the first row, their new baby boy in her arms. Little Mason the second.

He was only a few months older than Caroline, so I hoped they'd grow up inseparable friends. I looked at Dylan through my veil, a similar lace to my dress, and tried to blink away the tears when he lifted the panel that covered my face. Fuck, I hadn't realized how emotional that would make me.

I swiped at the tear that fell and beamed at him. "Hi."

"Hi there, beautiful."

"We can do this."

"We can do anything together, my dear. Come now, let's get married."

The rest was a blur until we kissed. That was when reality set in. I now had a thin gold band on my hand, all I'd wanted, and a husband kissing the world away. He'd wanted something finer, but I told him all I needed was him, and the chance to wear a pretty extravagant dress. And the chance to call him husband, of course. I didn't need a ring that cost more than some people made in a lifetime. I needed a thin gold band and a simple promise that he was mine, now and forever.

The guests cheered and I kissed his adoptive parents, thanked them for taking care of the man that I married, and for coming, and moved on as the crowd swept us along. Only, this time, instead of falling, I made it to the reception area that had been set up for our party. I found Caroline in my arms and a laugh on my lips.

"Oh, this is wonderful, Dylan. It was all I never dared to dream." I kissed him all over again as waiters brought food around to our guests.

"Well, my dear, from now on, no regrets, right? From the night we met, until now, I've had no regrets, and that's how I plan to live the rest of our lives." He kissed then grinned.

I could hardly wait for the moment he took the dress off of me, but it could wait. We had become used to waiting, and to be honest, finding little moments for some alone time had become almost a game that I really enjoyed. He was mine, and that was all that mattered.

We danced the night away, together, and with our family and friends. Roxie and Nathan came to take Caroline, her godchild, to bed, and Dylan and I quietly slipped away. We would leave in the morning for a honeymoon in Iceland. An odd choice, but when we talked about it, Dylan reminded me of the place I'd told him I always wanted to go. We'd made the arrangements. For tonight, Roxie and Nathan would keep Caroline for us, but tomorrow, we were going to jet off to an unknown land.

Right now, I just wanted to fall into bed with Dylan.

He pulled up against me as we rode the elevator up to the penthouse. I looked up at him. "Hello there, husband."

"Oh? No more sir?" he asked with a teasing glint in his eyes.

"If you'd like, of course, but I kind of like the sound of husband." I smirked up at him, and he ended the conversation with a kiss that took my breath away. My hair had been piled up on my head, but his fingers pushed pins out left and right.

Neither of us cared, we just kissed until the ride up was done. Then, hand in hand, he took me to our bedroom. With careful ease he undid every single button on my dress, until it fell to the floor. With strong arms Dylan picked me up and carried me to the bed.

My strapless bra soon disappeared, and the silk panties, the pair that he loved so much, only in bridal white, disappeared. He left the garter belt and the stockings on, though, I noted. "Like those, do you?"

"I do. It's so sensual." His fingers ran down my thighs to open them.

The hard ridge in his pants pressed into my center, and I wanted to feel him against my skin. I couldn't believe he still made me feel so weak, even after all of this time. "I think you need to get naked now, Dylan."

"As you wish, my dear," he whispered as I slid my hand down, ready to cup him in my palm. He tried to stop me, but I got up from the bed.

"As you wish, sir. Let me." I knelt beside him on the floor and used practiced fingers to remove his belt and slide down his zipper.

I looked up into his eyes as I pulled his cock from his pants. He pushed the pants down, and I pulled them away to throw them. They landed on the pile that was my wedding dress.

"Mm, I have waited all day for this," I whispered with wet lips along his shaft, before I sucked the thick head into my mouth. I loved doing this to him. The tight, silky skin was an addiction my tongue couldn't give up.

I ignored his moan even if it sent a shiver of excitement through me. I moaned to let him know I was there with him and eager for whatever he wanted to do.

"You fuck my head up so much, Emily." His words, an accusation, were said with a gentle, pleased tone. I knew he liked how I fucked his head up, and he wouldn't give it up for anything.

"I hope to fuck all of you before the night's over, Dylan, not just your head," I said with a sultry tone before I took all of him, until he stretched even my throat. It had taken some practice, but I'd learned to take all of him.

His hips thrust forward, and I felt him slide a little further down my throat; his gasp of pleasure a harsh sound. "That feels so fucking good, Emily."

I'd reply, but I was too busy concentrating on him. I wanted to wring far more than that from him. I pushed his thighs further apart and settled a hand over him as I pulled up off of his dick. His thigh muscles were hard against my sides, muscles that he worked hard to maintain. There'd been no sign of a flare at all over the last year, and we lived in silent hope that it would stay that way.

I used every trick I'd learned since the day I met him to tease Dylan. I thought he'd push me off of him, but instead, he thrust deeper, faster, until it felt as if my lips had gone numb from the pace, and he slid between them over and over. My need built as he pressed faster into my mouth, and I knew that if he came down my throat, it wouldn't be the end of this moment for us. We'd just been married. We had a lifetime to do this and so much more.

I squeezed my hand around him and felt him grow impossibly harder. I moaned around him, and he gasped and twisted above me, completely lost to how it felt to have me fuck him with my mouth.

"Are you wet, my sweet little wife?" he asked, his voice a harsh rasp that nearly made me get up off his dick to ride him. "You always did like blowing me like this. It makes you so wet.

"From the way you're gloating, I'd say you're just as satisfied as I am with the process." I narrowed my eyes and glared up at him. "But if you don't stop talking and let me finish what I'm doing, I'm going to make you find out just how wet I am."

"You know I'd be more than happy to do that." He pulled me up, and I wrapped my legs around his waist as he fell back on the bed.

Sometimes Dylan preferred to have me over him when he loved me like this, but today, I thought he wanted to feel the silk of my stockings against his face. I'd wanted to make him come in my mouth, but this was good too. We had forever, after all.

With eager but gentle fingers, he explored my silky skin while I propped myself up on my elbows to watch the show. I gasped when two long, thick fingers delved into me, just an exploration, though I wanted far more.

Dylan pulled the now slick fingers out of me, just as he slid his tongue along my throbbing clit. The fingers slid back in so slowly I wasn't sure they moved, until he had them completely inside of me.

My hips surged from the bed, and my desire turned into an inferno. I couldn't control myself and pressed my hips down to clench around his fingers, until he began to move the digits within me. The hot feel of his tongue against my sensitive skin nearly turned me inside out.

"Dylan. Fuck. Dylan!" I clenched at the duvet on the bed because I needed more. I needed him to make it all explode, somehow, someway. I knew he knew how to do it, he'd done it so very many times before.

Emotions flooded through me as I realized that he was my husband now, and it was okay to let him know just how much I loved him. Because he was more than just my husband; he was my love, and suddenly I wanted to burst with the weight of that love.

Instead, I came apart beneath him, around him. My body shook as his pace on me increased. The fingers inside of me stretched me, his tongue pressed into me faster, harder, and with a drive that pushed me over the edge. He knew what he was doing, he knew what he had caused within me, and I was sure I'd heard a gloating chuckle as my insides pulsed a wave of pleasure up to my brain.

Instead, he groaned as my hips writhed, his need almost beyond his control. I knew I'd have one more moment of bliss before he'd thrust into me, to drive us both over the edge all over again. I opened my legs, invited him in, and in seconds, he was there, inside of me fully.

"Fuck, that's so good!" Dylan was always pleased when he found his way inside of me. I clutched his shoulders as he surged down into me, his mind now focused on release, our release, not just his own. He wouldn't stop until he'd brought me with him. Although, to be fair, that didn't really take much with him.

We'd started out our lives together with a contract that could not stand to continue. We'd fought to maintain our control, we'd pushed against each other, and pushed each other away, despite how we needed each other. We'd done that until we were too tired to fight, and then we'd fought for our moment together some more. Now we were two people in love, and a family.

It amazed me and distracted me until I felt his muscles bunch in my hands. For once, I thought Dylan's control had slipped fully because I watched him grit his teeth, and I saw how his body moved, as if against his will, as he plunged into me with a groan.

"Emily, fuck baby. I can't hold on. I'm trying, but I'm not sure I can," he begged me to understand that he just couldn't hang on, and I did.

I leaned forward and captured his nipple in my mouth. I heard his breath as it hissed in between his teeth and knew that was the right move.

"Do that again," he demanded, and I answered that demand by sucking harder at the tiny nub. I decided if teasing one nipple caused that, then teasing both would be huge. I flicked at the other bud before I pinched it softly between the pads of my fingers.

"Fucking hell!" he cried out again and surged into me one last time. This time I felt the way he pulsed inside of me, and it made me greedy for my release. But it could wait. For the moment, I held him as he collapsed above me.

"I think we have to get married. So we can do this all over again, before you ask." He chuckled as he rolled away from me, too out of breath to say anymore.

"I'd marry you every day for the rest of my life, Dylan. But I don't think we have to take it exactly that far." I rolled over toward him and threw my leg over his thigh. I could wait for my pleasure now.

I wasn't that same girl, so eager and greedy, that I was when I met him. I knew what it meant to be loved, worshipped, and satisfied. I also knew that sometimes waiting made it far better when you got what you wanted. I'd waited most of my life for Dylan, and now I had him. And Caroline. I couldn't ask for anything more.

"I love you, Dylan," I whispered, as he rolled over to kiss me.

"I love you, Mrs. James. Until the end of my days."

DARK DESIRES
~ A billionaire dark romance series ~
Dark Desire
Dark Rules
Dark Secret
Dark Time
Dark Truth

BARRE TO BAR
~ A billionaire second chance series ~
Dancing With Lies
Dancing With Temptation
Dancing With Doubt
Dancing With Guilt
Dancing With Redemption

TWISTED INTENTION
~ A billionaire revenge romance series ~
Twisted Beauty
Twisted Love
Twisted Fate

Mafia's Obsession
~ A hot mafia romance series ~
Mafia's Dirty Secret
Mafia's Fake Bride
Mafia's Final Play

Screaming Demons
~ An MC romance series full of suspense ~
Rough Start
Rough Ride
Rough Choice
Rough Patch
Rough Return
Rough Road
Rough Trip
Rough Night
Rough Love

Standalone Contemporary Romance
Billionaire in Vegas
Billionaire Hunt

Billionaire's Game
Billionaire Retreat
Billionaire On Air
A Chance To Love
Somebody To Love
Not Mine To Love

Check out Summer's entire collection at
www.summercooper.com/books

ABOUT SUMMER COOPER

Thank you so much for reading. Without you, it wouldn't be possible for me to be a full-time author. I hope you enjoy reading my books as much as I do writing them.

Besides (obviously!) reading and writing, I also love cuddling my dogs, shouting at Alexa, being upside down (aka Yoga) and driving my family cray-cray!

Get in touch at
hello@summercooper.com
www.summercooper.com

facebook.com/summercooperauthor
instagram.com/summercooperauthor
goodreads.com/summercooper
bookbub.com/profile/summer-cooper

9 781917 075183